Like a Lover Never Leaving

Soul Treks into the Ultimate Love

By Jeremy A. Martin

CONTENTS

DEDICATION

For all those lovers
who have suffered

excruciating heartbreak
and thought they'd lost everything

only to discover
in the embrace of Divine Grace

the limitless River of Love
flowing within.

PREFACE

Part I: The Story

L *ike a Lover Never Leaving* has been a labor of love for ~~almost a~~ decade now. I could say this book took so long because of my demanding teaching schedule, my busy family life, or just my obsessive need to get the words right, but that's only part of the story. In truth, this manuscript needed all that time to bloom into its current form, which I can finally say I'm proud of. But what a long road to get here!

The seeds of this book were sown back in 2009, when a pair of intense dreams called me to the majestic mountains of Flagstaff, Arizona, for my first full-time teaching position. Those dreams told me it was time to wake up to my true destiny—right there, in the womb of the Desert Southwest—to use writing as a catalyst for healing, awakening, and transformation. With that new purpose in mind, I made my triumphant return to writing. After an eight-year-long dry spell.

That spell had finally been broken by Julia Cameron's classic book, *The Artist's Way: A Spiritual Path to Higher Creativity*, which reignited my love affair with writing. After reading her book and completing her Morning Pages, I began journaling and writing poems again; and then in the fall of 2009, I experienced an ecstatic epiphany.

While listening to Tiësto's *In Search of Sunrise 3*, I was inspired to write a scene about walking on a beach with Jesus Christ. Amidst the full moonlight, glittering sand, and rolling ocean waves, he taught me about the *Lover Never Leaving*, the Love of God we all carry within our own hearts. I didn't know it at the time, but the spiritual knowledge Christ passed on to me would end up in the book you're reading now.

Then, in March 2011, a month after my dad died, the inspiration for the novella hit. My father's death popped my own mortality bubble: I wondered, what am I waiting for? If not now, when? I knew with unwavering certainty I had to write this book—if not for others, at least for myself.

It took till about the third draft to realize this book would be a vessel for the lessons Christ taught me on that imagined beach, and it would take until 2015 to realize there was an instructional element to this project as well. I guess you could say I found my true spirituality from writing this book. I never knew it was there—just waiting for me—radiating and pulsating under the surface of my life.

I am so grateful for the divine gift of this book. It has impacted my life profoundly, and I can only hope it has a similar effect on you, Dear Reader.

Part II: The Structure

*L*ike *a Lover Never Leaving* has three distinct sections that are variations on the theme of longing for— and eventually finding—The Greatest Love There Is. I've arranged each section in a purposeful order, but you should feel free to start wherever your intuition guides you. What follows is an overview of the three parts of this book, so you can either read on to get some deeper insight into each part, or you can skip ahead to the first story in Trek I.

Trek I, *A Love Like Gravity*, offers a prelude to Dylan and Celeste's story in Trek II and is divided into two episodes. In Episode 1, a short memoir entitled "A Guilt Like Gravity," I share moments from my own life when I learned difficult lessons about what Love is—and what it isn't—with the help of some powerful teachers God sent my way. These teachers also happened to be some of my best friends and lovers, so I've changed their names to protect their identities. Ultimately, I'm grateful for the meaningful role they played in my life, and I pray they've forgiven me for any pain I've caused them. I want them to know how much I regret my actions, how much I've learned from those mistakes, and how their influence has helped me grow into a less selfish, more compassionate man as a result.

Episode 2, "A Perfect Astronomical Moment," tells the story of the most magical—yet most disillusioning relationship of my life—through the eyes of a character named Trystan Brennan. In this work of fiction, Trystan embarks on an inner journey to heal the loss of Wynter

Grey, the love of his life, and the woman who forever ruined romance for him. As he goes deeper into himself, he discovers the true Source of Love within, represented by Andalucía, a female spirit who appears in the final chapter of the novella that follows. The connections between Trystan and Dylan, Wynter and Celeste, are intentional and unavoidable. Their stories are two waves on the same ocean.

Trek II, *A Love Like the Tides*, is a novella that presents Dylan Hunter's search for the Ultimate Love in three chapters. Chapter 1, "A Love Like Drowning," opens up with Dylan facing the eight-year anniversary of Celeste Sorenson's rejection of his marriage proposal. Unable to cope with the memory of her ghost, he goes on a big drug binge that quickly spins out of control. Lost in the throes of a wicked acid trip, he meets a mysterious guide named Jeremiah Bolt, who opens the door to an opportunity he thought he would never get—a chance to see his Celeste one more time.

In Chapter 2, "A Love Like Lightening," Celeste invites Dylan to see her and her family over Easter weekend in Nelson, British Columbia, Canada. He jumps at the chance, hoping they will finally get back together after all this time. But Celeste has something completely different in mind: not romance, but reconciliation. She allows him to ask all the questions burning in his heart and mind since their breakup, and he begins to get the closure he has wanted for so long. And unbeknownst to him, she is harboring a secret surprise, one that will change his life forever.

Finally, in Chapter 3, "A Love Like Breathing," Dylan is tempted to head back to his hometown of Spokane, Washington, but a force he can't explain is keeping him in Nelson. That force guides him to a meditation center, where he embarks on the most incredible inner voyage. Leaving thoughts of Celeste far behind, he travels to a heavenly realm known as Empyrea and encounters Jeremiah Bolt again. As his tour guide, Bolt leads Dylan to meet three other supernatural guides—Judge Storm, The Advocate, and Andalucía—who take him on a profound journey into the center of his being to discover the Lover Who Will Never Leave Him.

Trek III, *A Love Like Igniting*, features 33 catalysts to spark deeper reflection and exploration of concepts dramatized in Treks I and II. I divided this part into four sections, like stages in a rocket, so as each stage is jettisoned, readers can be propelled into higher and deeper levels of understanding. Stage 1, "Countdown & Liftoff," introduces you to the foundational concepts of *Like a Lover Never Leaving*, reminding you of Love's true nature. Stage 2, "Breaking Free of Earth's Gravity," challenges you to leave behind the primal paradigm of mating and romance, and instead, to embrace a greater love led by your own spiritual evolution. Stage 3, "Entering Synchronous Orbit," illuminates the transformative path of relationships, and Stage 4, "Reentry into Paradise," shows you how to walk down that path with courage, creativity, and love. May each stage provide fuel for your own inner-space voyage!

I have also included a Soundtrack featuring all the songs and albums accompanying Treks I and II, and a Recommended Reading list with the books that laid the foundation for *Like a Lover Never Leaving*. These musicians and authors have been trusted companions on my long journey to create and complete this project, so I pray they will gift you with the same guidance, inspiration, and joy I have received from them.

Dear Reader, it is my ultimate hope that *Like a Lover Never Leaving* will remind you of this central truth: You don't have to look farther than your own heartbeat to discover the love you've always dreamed of. So please, breathe deeply and dive in! Your Inner Lover can't wait to welcome you home.

"Find the love you seek
by first finding the love
within yourself. Learn to rest
in that place within you
that is your true home."

— Sri Sri Ravi Shankar

TREK I:

A LOVE LIKE GRAVITY

EPISODE 1

A GUILT LIKE GRAVITY

On a mid-July night, my best friend Jacob and I go to a Christian rock concert. I think we're just going to enjoy a show, but I soon find out he has other intentions.

After the band finishes performing, the lead singer—a blond skinny kid with thick glasses, a black Slayer shirt and blue jeans—asks if anyone wants to come up and get "saved." I glance over at Jake. He nods for me to go up on stage. I shake my head and look away from him, down at the ground.

I'm pissed. This has all been a setup. I've always despised subterfuge. I want to get up and leave, but he's my ride, and I'm stuck here. And it's too far to walk home, especially on this rainy night.

Jake gets more insistent. He keeps whispering from across the aisle: "Go up there. Come on, dude, it'll be fine, I promise."

I still can't look at him. A few people get up to be saved, but I don't pay any attention to them. I'm too mad at Jake. Such deceit isn't very Christian.

Later, we're walking to his rusty gray Firebird, and he keeps asking why I didn't go up on stage. All I say is, "I didn't want to." After a while, he gives up.

Once in the car, we're quiet most of the ride home. Fittingly, R.E.M.'s "Losing My Religion" plays on the radio. Really, God? You're shaming me too? I can't believe it. Is the entire universe conspiring against me?

The tenor of our friendship forever changed after that night. I never got saved, and Jake never asked me again. He knew he'd crossed a line, and there was no going back. He knew he'd betrayed me.

Then, a couple months later, he betrays himself. On our way to our cars after school one day, he asks me, "Guess what I lost?"

"What, your car keys?" I reply sarcastically.

"No man, it begins with a V."

Aren't "saved" people supposed to "save" themselves for marriage? Guess not.

Who's really the spiritual one here?

The following summer, we're hanging out in our old high school parking lot again. I'm in college, he's in the Army. I've changed. He hasn't.

"So man, you still the Big V?" he asks derisively.

"Yeah, but I've still kissed a lot of girls, though."

He snickers. "Yeah, so did I. In fifth grade."

"Hey man, I'm just waiting for the right girl to come along. I want it to mean something, you know?"

More laughter in my face. "Dude, the right girl is the one right now. You just need to get as much action as you can before you settle down and get married. Stop trying to make it special. Sex is fun, but it don't mean shit."

I go to open my mouth, but think better of it. Now I realize we're from two different worlds. And always will be. After that day, we never see each other again.

I guess the good news is he ends up knocking up some girl in the Army, while I end up marrying a woman who remained the Big V until our wedding night.

Huh. I guess fate is the best revenge.

* * *

In the shower, Melanie's sobbing. I head out the door to buy a pregnancy test, and even though it might be too early to tell, I still need the reassurance. If this is what having sex is like, maybe it's not worth it.

Because with Mel, everything is different. And more complicated. Now that I'm no longer the Big V.

To our great relief, the test is negative, and we talk about it. "Maybe we should stop having sex for a while," she says. I nod, somewhat agreeing.

Of course, a week later, we're back at it. But something between us has changed. We're not more careful, as you might think, but more tentative, more unsure of our connection. Looking back, I realize it was the death knell of our relationship. My exodus across the country was my need to get away from her. I think she sensed it. We only survive until the following spring, when our love stops bearing fruit.

"I got caught up in it," she says.

Wow, if this is what love is like, then I want nothing to do with it.

Our breakup is tacit, tactless. Listening to Live's "Run to the Water," I weep.

I run, run, run, vainly trying to catch up to what we had the previous year. But in bed that night, she picks her nose, mutters. I just stare at the ceiling, knowing I'm trapped in some kind of nightmare.

When I wake up, we've already withered. The next love—on purpose—would be tepid and safe, a haven from love's storms.

But when the shelter collapses, I implode. This is when I adopt the philosophy that love is a planned demolition. It's best to keep a safe distance.

That's when the countdown begins.

* * *

Midnight strikes on New Year's Eve, and the drunken threshold has been passed. It's on.

I black out for a bit. When I come to, Ashlynn and I are making out. And we can't stop. We're two desperate, lonely people, needing something, if not each other. We kiss in the club, oblivious to all around us; in the cab, unabashedly not caring about others looking on; in the hotel, naked from the waist up. We don't have sex that night, but believe me, I try.

Because at this point, as Jake would say, I'm still the "Big V." My first time with Melanie is still months away.

The next morning after we wake up, Ashlynn's in the shower washing me off, and I'm just staring at the ceiling, still feeling the gravity of her kiss on my lips. Before we head back home, we talk in the parking lot outside our hotel room. I ask her if this is just a drunken mistake, just lust taking us over. She insists it isn't. I struggle to believe her.

For the remaining nights on my Christmas break, the passion is off the charts. She's the first woman to ever give me an orgasm, and she is hands down one of the best kissers ever. Fittingly, Louis Armstrong's "A Kiss to Build a Dream On" becomes our signature song.

She even lets me meet her seven-year-old daughter from a previous relationship. I'm normally not very good with kids, but we hit it off right away—playing, laughing, having fun. I soon realize Ashlynn and her girl could be my family. They could be my future.

But that future never materializes. I make damn sure of that.

As soon as I return to my college 800 miles away, I stop communicating with Ashlynn. I try to rationalize: I don't want to stay in my hometown; I don't want to be a stepdad. But those are just excuses. The real truth—as it has always been—is I'm scared to death of the real love she represents.

When I don't respond to her calls or emails, she sends me a nasty letter. Even though Melanie defends me, saying she would gather a parade of support for me, I still feel guilty.

And looking back on it, I deserved every scathing word. I was the asshole I'd so often condemned. The one who throws women away callously and doesn't look back. Until the guilt's too much.

That Kiss to Build a Dream On had died. And it was all my fault.

* * *

On Easter Sunday, I need a resurrection, even if artificially produced.

Just like usual, it takes exactly half hour for the sacrament to kick in. And this time, it's an Omega, a strongly dosed pill. What did Jesus say about being the Alpha and the Omega?

The pleasure is orgasmic, like God has pried open my sternum with his divine crowbar, unveiling my beating heart for all to see. Instead of feeling afraid, or exposed, I feel powerful. I feel free.

So this is what it feels like to be alive.

Throughout the evening, Evie tries to keep up with me by smoking marijuana, but she can't. I'm off in space while she's still trying to break free of Earth's gravity—an unfair race from the start.

I take some Mardi Gras beads from the floor, arrange them into galaxy spirals, then turn them into octopus arms, explaining how their bodies can change colors to express various moods. While life energy flows through me unabated, I feel like an immortal child, playing the universe into existence.

As I laugh, she looks both awed and terrified. I know how she feels. That's how God makes me feel too.

At one point, she gets up to check on her toddler daughter, who just cried out. I wonder if she knows what we're up to, or at least senses something isn't right.

With her gone for a few minutes, my thoughts turn inward, like the bead pinwheel I've just made. I realize I have an unhealthy attitude toward Jesus Christ, not because of some personal bias, but because of the way other people—like Jake—have distorted my own thinking about Him. Interesting that my thoughts turn to Jesus on Easter. Hmm, I wonder if He's behind all this.

Going deeper, I realize all the suffering in my life is based on one main problem: my lack of love, both for myself and others. I don't understand all the implications of this epiphany, but it's beginning to make sense. It also makes sense that since I've divorced myself from Christ, there would be a lack of love in my life.

As if to demonstrate this, Evie comes back, having settled her daughter down and gotten her back to sleep. We begin a discussion about our relationship, how it's both platonic and romantic. She says we could be more, but I'm holding back. And she's right. Holding back is what I do best.

When I give her a list of reasons why we wouldn't work, none of them are convincing—least of all to me— and no amount of explanation or apology can bring us back. Our friendship doesn't last too much longer after that. She goes back to being with her ex-boyfriend—who soon becomes my ex-best-friend—and I go back to being alone, where I'm most comfortable.

Hmm. Here's another relationship that could've been something, but wasn't, all thanks to my shit. Ok Jesus, I see now. Your timing, as always, is perfect. My lack of love, along with all my insecurities and fears, has impeded another romantic, perhaps spiritual connection.

Talk about a sobering comedown.

* * *

At a healing arts school, the class talks about Jesus's crucifixion, and a volunteer has to get into the pose, as we all do. (We all know this by heart, don't we?) I don't know why, but my heart is pounding, and I can't slow it down. It knows the urgency of the moment all too well.

Now I realize Christ wasn't really crucified. Humanity was. Wow. I start thinking about the ways I have put Him on the cross, while I enjoyed watching Him writhe in pain. But wait. Or is it me writhing in pain on the cross, as Christ watches me, wondering why I've refused His offer of Divine Love? The answer, at this point, seems obvious.

On the drive home that Sunday, I'm behind a big-rig truck, and someone has dust-written *John 3:16* on the rear door of its trailer. When I look up the Bible verse later, its words are piercingly familiar: "For God so loved the world that he gave his one and only Son, that whoever believes in him shall not perish, but have eternal life."

Ok God. I'm starting to get the message.

* * *

Christina has a refrigerator magnet that says, "Jesus is Lord." My God, I can't get away from it. Or should I say, from Him. He's relentless.

Chrissy looks like Melanie—the one who stole my Big V; the one who uttered those infamous words: "I got caught up in it." I assume the resemblance is intentional. In her face I see the deep depression I carry from my lack of love, from my Divine Divorce.

I do everything I can to run away.

When we break up, she threatens to kill herself. That gets my attention, but I still don't want to be with her. I visit her in the psychiatric ward of the hospital, and it's like I'm visiting part of myself in there. We kiss, but her breath tastes medicinal.

I realize she's the sane one, actually admitting she needs help. In truth, I'm the crazy one, blindly and boldly believing that I don't need help, that I can go it on my own. I didn't see the irony then, but I see it now.

Her friend is there too, and she shoots me a death look.

I know, I know. I should feel guilty about this.

And I do.

* * *

In her house, Ruth and I smoke up before anything else happens, as if we need our minds altered to do what's been in the back of our minds ever since we became friends. The foreplay is some of the sweetest I've ever experienced: We kiss and caress, then stop to talk and laugh—with each wave of love, we open up more, go deeper. It feels natural, relaxed. We take our time.

But paradoxically, the moment soon arrives. She lets me go in bare at first, but when I get close to coming, she says, "Are you sure?"

Dear God no. When it comes to love, and the real Big V—Vulnerability—I never am.

So I put on my protection, charge ahead anyway.

Afterward, we cuddle up together, our conversation amped up to the next level. That's when it hits me—sex is not the end, but the beginning. It's spiritual foreplay.

The next morning, in the light of day, we return to just being friends. Our conversation during breakfast is like it always is—deep, but somehow stripped of its nocturnal magic. We don't talk about the dinosaur in the room, but she knows. She always knows what's going on inside me. And that's what scares me to death.

To bury the fear, I treat our coming together as a one-night stand. It's the only way I can face it. I don't even call her later that day, but when we do talk, she's pissed.

And she had every right to be. I'd rejected her, her three children, her love unconditional. All because she didn't fit my preconceived image of the One. All because I was terrified of becoming a father and husband. And most of all, because I just couldn't accept this truth: that Romance is nothing but an illusion, a costume we dress around Love's Great Light.

Little did I know, contained in that Great Light is the Ultimate Lover—the one who will always love me and never leave me. But that truth wasn't even a glimmer in my imagination. I still had to experience more heartache and heartbreak, more loss and longing, before I could let go of all my romantic illusions.

And I wasn't there yet. Not by a long shot.

EPISODE 2

A PERFECT
ASTRONOMICAL MOMENT

Early morning, another party's over. The sun rises mutely through black blinds, shining on the smoke-smelly couch, the air conditioner blasting. All my so-called friends are sleeping, while I'm wide awake, restless.

Slowly the drugs wear off, and the emptiness blows in, like an unwelcome wind. It fills me up like a toxic balloon, and I yearn for bursting, or at least deflation. But once a universe is created, there's no stopping it.

I just lie there, adrift, distant, like I always am. The only punctuation for this noisy silence is my blinking, a nervous tic. I don't know why I keep doing this. Riding the rollercoaster of neurotransmitters is always a dangerous ride, an evil game of diminishing returns—the higher I fly, the harder I fall. Simple physics. I'm gravity's bitch.

A thought intrudes: *What is this emptiness?*

It's an ancient grief, the loss of the One, rippling through the placid lake of time. My breathing inflates it, and I go along for the ride. Yet again.

* * *

Sitting in the dark of my car, I'm listening to Collective Soul's "The World I Know."

Without warning, a lifetime of loneliness hits me—all at once—and I can't hold back the tears. The dam has finally broken.

It's hard to breathe through the sobs.

I pray, something I haven't done in years, but now my desperation has reached its zenith: "Please, God . . . send me someone to love."

There it is, out there, like a transmitted radio signal, and there's no taking it back. The red light on top of The Kissing Tower flashes, as if receiving my communiqué. I smile. Maybe now, the waves of love will get rolling.

I roll down the windows, chocolate wafting in. It's ironic. I live in the so-called "Sweetest Place on Earth," but life here has been sour and bitter without love, without shining and singing in SHE. I'm a long-distance runner, but even for me, the space is too much.

"The World" fades out to something unimportant, like a commercial, or a DJ rambling on, so I switch the radio off: No more static; no more stasis. For now, I want silence. This sacred silence.

Coming home, all the green lights blink awake.

* * *

I remember that night—shining like millions of stars, filling up like billions of balloons. A perfect astronomical moment. Being pulled by gravity, again.

There she is, lighting up her front porch. In Wynter's eyes is a cosmos too large, too distant to reach. Yet somehow our spheres connect, now thinly tethered, their threads tightening. Our kiss begins and ends in a blink, but its effects are long lasting.

I'm flying again in my car, the wind blasting through open windows, louder than any music I've ever heard. For once, my stereo is dark, mute. I just want it to be about this feeling, this silence, unshaded by notes and beats.

So this is what it feels like, this forever floating, this raft to shore against the emptiness. I'm free to explore at will now, after the most sublime touching of lips.

* * *

Wynter's kiss sparks explosions in my brain, igniting internal combustion, as the engine of her body pistons fast against mine. Her mouth is agape, her hips reckless. As she drives me over the edge, I plummet, our bodies sunless, yet incandescent.

When we emerge again from deep waters, sunrays stream through stained glass, our bodies siphoning light. Now illuminated, we speak sweetly, laugh often.

In Wynter's embrace, I've found paradise. And in this moment, I realize I want this—nothing but this—for the rest of my days.

* * *

"Do you believe in guardian angels?" she asks me, as we climb over the locked gates to the Gardens, an echo of Eden forgotten. Our feet hit the ground with a suppressed thud.

We are alone and quiet contained.

"The trees are beautiful, aren't they?" Wynter's voice cuts through the silence like ice.

I strain to look at the pines. Their needle branches splice the celestial underbelly of cloud, as indigo peeks in, a reminder of winter.

Yet we are impervious to the cold.

Our pupils lock—portals to another world. We descend onto the snow to make a connected snow angel, and when we ascend again, Wynter's still stargazing. She nods, smiling at my affirmative answer. We trudge to a bridge where the gleaming white coalesces all around us.

As the stream courses underneath, we flow together, ice crackling.

In water's frozen mirror, I see myself walking alone in December snow, full moonlight glittering a path for me to follow. There is only one pair of footprints.

I pray it's because I'm carrying her.

I reach out for her hand, but she's already running. Wynter's sleek form navigates the cold too easily, and I can't catch her before she crosses the finish line to my car. As we run into our penultimate embrace, our hearts hammer desperately at our ribcages.

I yearn for us to shatter into the other.

* * *

By the fireplace, our fragile lovemaking is spiritual foreplay. The fire dances on the periphery of her irises, but in the center, I burn brightly inside. I have never seen myself so clearly in someone, like staring into the pupils of God.

"Your eyes are a perfect mirror," she says. "I can see our universe in them."

I blink back tears, incendiary. The fire, her flesh, the scorching connection of our eyes—it's all too much. But Wynter doesn't let up. Her intensity is relentless: "I feel like I'm melting into you."

I want to let go, but I can't. In my mind, oneness means annihilation. Love equals death.

She catches my retreat before I do. When the fire vacuums out of her eyes, she says, "You have such a profound sadness, Trystan. I don't know if even I can reach it."

I collapse like a neutron star into her.

* * *

David Holmes's "Gone" floats over the air conditioners, a soundtrack for this profound loneliness. As if no one is sleeping in the adjacent rooms. As if this whole apartment building, this entire street block and city, have been abandoned. My thoughts only increase the separation. My "friends" must've put this music on just to torture me, just to give me the nightmares haunting their sober brains.

Still ruminating, still sinking or lifting, I can't tell. I don't think the direction matters. What matters is this paradox, this fullness within the emptiness, gnawing on my cortex like a meal of worms.

Am I dead? Have I left my body?

I look down, touch my limbs. Still here. Still seem real. Unless I'm hallucinating again. If so, might as well enjoy the ride.

When I let go, I hear a snapping sound, then a voice: *You are full of a lack of love. You must drain it to be free.*
I brace myself, laughing and flying into the shining ether.

* * *

One day after full moon, its light a thick red, a hemorrhage in the darkness. Its reflection on the nearby pond evokes a cacophony of crickets, cicadas, and frogs. For once, the roads are still, but I am not.
It is the most maddening peace I have ever felt.
I sit cross-legged in the damp grass, feel its needle wetness seep slowly through my skin, as I watch fireflies launch into the air like phosphorescent airplanes. They flash yellow-green at a languid pace—pulsing light in one dimension, blinking dark in another. A chill saturates my spine; even my cells quiver.
So this is how the longing began. The longing for someone or something else. For a connection beyond the mundane.
Manure lingers in the air, and I put my head to my bent knees, holding my breath.
I fall back into the dank ground to be absorbed. The longing rests in a place beyond sleep, beyond dream, somewhere in the void that created darkness and light.
Dawn telegraphs its arrival with faint wisps of lustrous blush, as dandelions sprout into my scalp, planting sunlight in my hair. I am reborn into the next stage.

* * *

The morning is a creature humming alive—fog exhales diffused sunlight onto the road; air pulses with the anticipation of fall.

But dawn is also aware of its beckoning dormancy. The incoming chill has diminished the insect song, and even the pungent odor of fertilizer has been muted. Decay is the dominant scent now.

The streetlights buzz and appear glossed over, their jaundiced eyes creaking open for the beginning of another day. As always, I'm reluctant to let the light in.

Then, Wynter's eyes penetrate the fog. They are as green as I remember them. They still have those brown specks like keyholes. She stares through me, my blueness breaking off inside the lock.

So this is what it feels like to exist.

Though running half-asleep, I ascend the hill into that expanding hum.

* * *

A blink, a particle of light, and it's just me. The road is made for the rubber of shoes, not the rubber of tires. If you want to be deliberate, miles per hour is too fast to feel yourself.

The double yellow line stretches out like a rope bridge into the dawn, heatwaves of silent music rippling around me.

The moon surrenders to this tyranny of sun, this blotting out of my quiet comforting dark, my asylum of stars. In the shadows I am free to be; yet in the light everyone can see me, exposed, like an overdeveloped photograph.

I stand—blinking—a transparent of the moment. Yes, I miss her. And you know what? She's not coming back.

* * *

A guttural cry howls into the winter womb, claws its way through my throat, till I am raw, stumbling to my car, drunk from heartbreak.

The door to Wynter's house whimpers shut, the blinds dropping behind me. Finally, a lamp shuts off. I hope she's crying, but more likely, she's going to sleep to forget me.

Later that night in my cold bed, I can only sleep to remember her, dreaming of a defiant spring.

Snow melts into green grass; swirling leaves repopulate the trees; fruit funnels out of exploding blossoms. As the rains arrive wistfully, the sun bursts behind me, its rays filling me up with liquid light.

I welcome my return to this luminous saturation.

Just before I drown, a woman reaches out, embraces me with her rainbow arms. My eyelids flutter, her face glows orange.

My God, there are two setting suns.

I am Andalucía, she who walks in the light. I am love coalesced. Let me lighten your burden, dear lover.

Lifting me out of the Earth's placenta, she cradles my face next to hers, her smile a hopeful sunrise. She sings in a high G, rocking me back and forth—until we are one wetness, one vibration, one voice—singing against the inky palette of this incessant night.

Our symphony of stars swells into celestial tune.

* * *

We stare at the indigo cornea above us, viewing and contemplating infinity—our hands constellated, our heads colliding planets. The Perseid meteor shower rains ceaselessly over us, like skydivers plummeting through the atmosphere, their spirits blazing on the way down.

We brace for impact.

"I feel like we're the only two people in the universe right now," she declares, her voice ignited by love.

Wynter sighs like the Big Bang. She rolls her head toward me, kisses my neck softly; then her breathing slows, she falls asleep. Her brain reflects tonight's sky—neurons fire like shooting stars of dream and thought, while images of me surf neurotransmitters, crashing into the shores of her dead synapses.

I pray this moment will always exist, no matter what dimension we're in. Smiling like the crescent moon, I turn my face to kiss her. Wynter stirs, kisses back. Her arms wrap around me—celestially wide, gravity close.

Orion, leering over the horizon, attends to winter.

* * *

"Isn't it magical?" Wynter whispers.

"What did you say?"

"I said, isn't it magical? The way the snow and sun are glowing together, like they're being baked in an oven."

"That's so weird. I was just thinking that."

"Well, that's no surprise," she says, cradling my face with her soft hands. "We've always been in sync, ever since we first met."

Wynter pulls me closer as we hike up to the summit.

We aren't prepared for the surreal view at the lookout point. Down below, the radio towers' red lights flash intermittently, rhythmically, lulling us into a trance. The pine trees, suffused with a warm glow, ignite every crystal of snow in winter wildfire. We just stand there— mouths agape—watching the sunset deepen to magenta, then purple.

"It's like looking inside the heart of God," she proclaims, again reading my mind. From the sunset, her body is bathed in dancing orange and blue, like some kind of eternal flame.

We turn to face each other, and then slowly, tentatively, we lean in for our first kiss. As soon as our lips touch, we're electrified, incandescent. When we finally pull back to look at each other, my heart is racing.

"Oh my God, Trystan!" Placing her hand over her mouth, her eyes shine like contained lightning.

* * *

Heat lightning detonates throughout the blue vascular sky, flickering in the back of my retinas. Though it's mute and on the horizon behind me, the storm threatens to wrap around again with thunderous tenacity.

When I imagine Wynter's face, her naked and skim-milk body on our bed, lightning surges through my veins. Still running, I charge forward.

Flashing to our first night making love. Red emergency sirens penetrate the dusty blinds of my apartment's windows, coating our skin with warning. We kiss and caress, quiver and flutter, soar as breathless pulsars; then we cry out into the night, our longing sated—at long last. After, we bask in the heat of our thrumming bodies.

As our tremors subside, she says she feels stars in her fingertips. Wynter touches my forehead and sighs.

* * *

Another night touches my heart. We're in her car, after work. She climbs out of the driver's seat, fills up my passenger side. Wynter gives me her warm breathing body, but nothing else.

Something is missing. I hold her body firm, but I let her soul drop into the earth. Such a love cannot be held too long, for fear of crushed wings.

When I finally let her go, her car drives off without me, the road chewed up in pieces, another animal parting. The internal roar is deafening.

* * *

Thunder drums itself back into my existence, lightning retreating. Rain mixes with motor oil, slicks the streets in swirling rainbow, steeping me in patterns of concentric sadness.

As I pass a discarded windshield on the shoulder of the road, the glass of her shatters into me, shards shooting through my pores like daggers.

Such fragility reminds me of the diamond engagement ring I gave Wynter. By the time I turn the corner—sprinting into the home stretch—her rejection cuts right through me.

"I'm being unfair to you," she says, slipping the ring back into my coat pocket like a magician.

I want to rant about the injustice of it all, but I know any attempt to win her back is futile. Her mind is already made up. "I should go," is all I say.

I walk out to the kitchen, pregnant with antiques, and suddenly, I feel obsolete. She's still holding one of my hands, but when she finally lets go, it falls like a heavy pendulum. The zipper of my coat emits a high pitch of protest.

At the front door, next to the now dormant fireplace, I turn to face her. Wynter holds me in her gaze, and I can't break free. I don't want to leave her solar system and its alluring gravity.

I peer deep into her irises, supernovae frozen in mid-explosion. "I want to make you the center of my universe."

By the time she returns my gaze, there are already parsecs between us. "But Trystan, *you* should be the center of *your own* universe."

I nod, wrapping my galaxy arms around her, while she weeps, her tears like miniature suns burning into my skin.

A forever has never been so painfully finite.

When I step back into the dark December snow, it still glitters in the faint moonlight, prodding me to look up. A diamond road sign seems to scream "Dead End."

How prophetic. How pathetic.

How did I miss such an obvious omen?

The Universe responds with a shooting star—streaking across the indigo eyelid of night—sparking an internal fire.

In that moment, all I can do is pray for resurrection.

* * *

Back in my car, I am disconsolate. I thought I had found the One. But now I have nothing.

I have never felt heartbreak like this. Then again, I've never opened myself up to loving someone this much either. Now I see why I didn't. It's just too painful.

Fittingly, Fuel's "Hemorrhage" plays on the radio. My heart rages, my throat keens in tune.

I stare down this Dead End road with blurry eyes. *Are you happy, God? Is that why you orchestrated this moment, just so I'd be here for this song? Do you like seeing me suffer? Don't I deserve to be happy?*

Then it hits me. Oh yeah, I'm doing this to myself, with what I call the Icarus Maneuver. At the first sign of sunlight I take off, careening toward the source of warmth—not realizing, until it's too late—that my wings are melting. Now I'm condemned, plummeting back to Earth.

Gravity's bitch, again.

Sweet Jesus, Earth is Love Boot Camp. You have to master the basics before you can move on to more advanced training. Before you can graduate from kindergarten in God's School of Love.

But damn. Why does it have to be so fucking hard?

TREK II:

A LOVE LIKE
THE TIDES

1

A LOVE LIKE DROWNING

It's my anam cara[1] and me. The way it's always been. The way it's meant to be.

We coast down Celtic streets, singing verses from "Just Like Heaven." I can't stop staring at her. Her hair glows gold in the sunlight; her eyes radiate aquamarine.

A claddagh ring with a sapphire heart shines through the display window of the Divine Diamond, its facets blinding us. In a flash, we're inside the jewelry store, staring at the ring. As soon as I point to it, she's beaming.

"Oh Dylie, it's beautiful."

"I'll take that one!"

The clerk, an old but youthful-looking woman dressed in turquoise, slides open the glass counter. "This ring was made in the Isle of Skye, representing the infinite blue of spiritual love. Once you're submerged in its deep waters, you'll never come up for air again."

---

[1] *Anam Cara* is a Celtic term for "soul companion." I use this word instead of "soulmate" because it connotes more of a spiritual connection that does not have to be romantic.

Her expression is unfathomable. I just nod, handing her the money in gold coins.

"She must be a very special lady to receive such a ring."

"Yes, she has my heart completely."

"And that's not all she has a grip on, dear Icarus."

Her face turns sinister, so I take the ring, grab my lover's hand, and we hurry out of the store. Under a womb-like sky, I slide her ring on. Her smile eclipses the sun.

After another flash, we're on the Cliffs of Moher, watching the rolling waves crash against the shore. While we embrace and kiss softly, I dive into her eyes, splash inside her irises.

Plunging into cold water, I go numb, sinking deeper and deeper, unable to swim toward the surface, sunlight retreating further and further from my vision. Her hand reaches out, but it's all in vain.

The Cure sings our dirge, as the flange guitars of The Cranberries' "Zombie" flood my head, filling it with a buzzing bends.

I bubble out of my body, watching my face freeze into a silent scream. Soon, darkness envelops me, my lover's claddagh ring swallowed by the murky depth of the ocean floor.

Ω

I shot up awake—choking, my heart pounding—like actually drowning. When I finally caught my breath, I cried out, "Celeste! Oh my God, Celeste!"

As I buried my face in my pillow, the tears came unbidden. The Celeste dreams had returned.

"Goddammit!" I raged, punching the mattress several times, wanting to knock out the past—this time, for good.

Throwing off the covers and tumbling out of bed, I sighed. I knew I shouldn't have slept in those blood-red sheets, but I couldn't help it. Today was the eight-year anniversary of Bad Friday—March 21, 2008—the date of Celeste's Ultimate Rejection of my marriage proposal. To sleep in anything else for that occasion seemed sacrilegious.

I opened the dusty blinds, watched the rain streak down. Images of Celeste's svelte and tender face stormed into my mind—her eyes cobalt lightning—like a strobe light I couldn't shut off. Her eyelids fluttered, dreaming of the paradise we had once created together.

Ω

"This is Edenic, isn't it?" Celeste says. "It's like we're Adam and Eve, and no one else is around."

"You know, I bet Adam and Eve had lots of sex," I said. "I mean, what else would they do?"

"Yeah, and God was just watching them that whole time, like some kind of pervert."

Giggling, she pulls the red sheets over us as a protective shell. "I wouldn't want God to get any ideas."

"I know, right?" I say, snuggling closer to her. "But ya know, Celeste, if he really wanted to, he could just peer through this blanket, no problem. He is God after all."

"What? I don't think so. He doesn't have X-ray vision. He's not Superman, for Christ's sake."

Our laughter collapses into our kiss. Her teeth tug at my bottom lip.

"I want you, Dylie. Forever."

Eyes closed, we explode awake.

Lightning flashes into my heart, charging headlong and swirling inside capillary beds, our blood raging into the storm again. We rush into our sanctuary of flesh and limbs, fingers and toes, tongues and lips and teeth, and I can't tell where I end and she begins, a river of light winding through the fertile soil of our souls.

Ω

My head still swimming, I stared at the blue glow of my alarm clock. 3:33. *Damn.* I knew I wouldn't be sleeping tonight . . . again. So I did what I always did when insomnia struck—I called Jules.

She picked up before the second ring. "Hey D, what's up?"

"Oh, you're still awake?"

"Come on, D, you know I'm a night owl." As she made hooting noises into the phone, I rolled my eyes. "The question is, what're you doing up so late? Insomnia again?"

"Yep."

"You're not partying without me, are you?"

Her disappointment was palpable. "Actually Jules, that's why I'm callin'. I wanted to see if I could come over."

"You know you don't have to ask, D."

"I know, but guess what? I got some pills. You wanna roll tonight?"

"Hmm, let me see . . . of course I wanna fuckin' roll. You kiddin' me?"

"That's what I thought. See ya soon, Jules."

"Fly, don't drive, D."

Thank God her Altura apartment was only half a mile away. Any farther and I might burst. I was dying to get high again.

I threw on my *Brand New Day* T-shirt, slipped on my favorite holey jeans, grabbed my party kit full of pills and potions, and flew out the door into the Spokane rain.

Ω

As soon as I arrived at the door to Julie's apartment, I stopped, closed my eyes, took a deep breath. There, beyond that threshold, lay a gateway to another world. A more blissful world. I opened my eyes, glided inside.

When I walked in, cinnamon incense was burning, and she was all lit up, the freckles on her cheeks almost glowing. I chuckled. She couldn't wait to take the sacrament either.

Her approach was always like a sigh of relief—that frizzy auburn hair, those pale green eyes, those sensuous lips, that electric smile. I watched her bare feet and purple-painted toenails as she sashayed toward me, pressing her curvy body into mine.

I loved Jules because she was absolutely nothing like Celeste. Being with her was a welcome break from Celeste's ghost.

"You got the beans?" she asked excitedly.

"Yep. Care to see the vintage?"

"You bet. Don't tease me anymore."

I pulled out a small baggie with the pills. "Only two?" she said with a mock frown.

"Look again."

She peered closer. "Ooh, they're Omegas. So we *are* going to have a good time tonight, aren't we?"

"You know the sky's the limit with you, Jules."

"I've been looking forward to this since the last time we rolled." As she parachuted the pill, I jumped out of the airplane with her.

She yanked me into the living room like a ripcord, and we landed on her leather couch in a pile of limbs. Once again, I noticed her poster imprinted with a psychedelic tree of life. It was the only gift of mine she had on display.

We stared at the design for what seemed like a long time, listening to the rain patter outside. Meaningless images flickered on the TV, hypnotizing me until the chemicals kicked in.

"Ooh, I almost forgot the music," she cooed. "How about some *In Search of Sunrise 3*?"

"Tiësto? That's the perfect rolling album."

"I know, right?" She pressed play on her remote, dimmed the halogen lamp, turned off the TV. "Let the journey begin!"

The first track, "Into the Fire," washed over me like waves on a beach. Heat and tingling radiated from my chest through my stomach, into my legs, and out my toes. The other wave shot up to my head—neurons exploding like fireworks—serotonin sailing across synapses. It felt like someone had broken open my ribcage, exposing my heart to the entire universe. I rolled my head back, moaning, "Oh my God!"

"Feels *so damn good*, doesn't it, D?" she said, extracting the exquisite juice out of each word.

Jules was inside my head again, listening to my thoughts; then she was inside my heart, piggybacking on my pulse. My spirit charged toward her like unleashed electricity.

She reached out, reading the chillbump Braille on my forearms. "Whoa, you're in it deep, aren't you? Tell me what you're thinking."

I stared at her smiling face, watching her eyes bugging out as she struggled to focus on me. "I just realized how much I love you."

Instantly, a chasm of silence opened up between us.

"Do you know how long I've been waiting to hear you say that?"

I tried to think, but my cerebrospinal fluid had already ignited like jet fuel. "Uh . . . a long time?"

She squeezed my hand. "It's been over two years, but I'll forgive you. You just better remember next time!"

We laughed, stripping down to our underwear. I relished the red, silky lace fabric of her bra and panties. "Wow Jules, I'm likin' the lingerie."

"I wore it just for you, D." Her full weight fell on me as we pushed our arms out, interlacing our fingers. Her curly hair rained down on my face, her kiss dragging me under in a powerful current.

"I've been waiting so long for you to say that. Not knowing how you really felt was killing me inside."

"I know, Jules, I know. And I'm sorry for that. I don't know why I've been hiding my feelings from you all this time."

"Well, it was worth the wait. And now that I have you, I'm never letting you go. I love you too damn much." She unhooked her bra, tossed it to the floor. "Take your boxers off."

Once naked, our bodies were furnaces, blasting through the pores of our skin.

Time passed in strobe-light flashes.

"Let's sit up," she said tenderly. "I want to embrace all of you."

We kissed, our lips following the flow of the music, her heart thumping against my chest.

"I see all of you Dylan, and I love every part," she said, her green eyes brightening. "I love you so much, more than I've ever loved anyone."

She said this from such a deep place, that same place where I used to say "I love you" to Celeste. And now, instead of loving her back, I just sat there, pulling away, exactly like Celeste had done, all those years ago.

It just wasn't fair.

Ω

A mash-up of Sinead O'Connor's "Nothing Compares 2 U" and Conjure One's "Tears from the Moon" floats like a ghost, shadowing me down a dark hallway. I rush into my boyhood bedroom—formidable winds blowing me toward an inevitable destination—where I find the most unexpected, but most welcome guest.

It's Celeste.

She stands there, dressed solely in her astral body, staring through me. Her blue eyes and blonde hair have dulled to grey, her expression blank, almost lifeless. She isn't even smiling.

"Dylan, you have to let me go."

"But I can't. You're my everything!"

"Then I can't be held responsible if you destroy your life."

She frowns, her body fading to shadow. Her chakras turn on, illuminating the room, then churn together into an expanding cyclone, her eyes glowing hot in the storm's center.

Inside her pupils spins a turntable, a diamond needle playing James Holden's "I Have Put Out the Light."

Just then, the power goes out; the cyclone implodes. Silence bursts into my ears. Moonlight filters through the blinds, one degree at a time, while I await Celeste's return. But it's no use. She's gone forever—swept away by an indifferent storm.

Ω

As the dream storm subsided, Julie and I began to come down, passing a joint back and forth. We stared at the popcorn ceiling, the chill music of Kruder and Dorfmeister tracing patterns on its white surface. First came the swirl of black dots, moving like a swarm of gnats; then the pattern began to descend and extend into spiders, their spindly legs cascading down like confetti streamers, wrapping me in webs of disembodied thought.

Before I could drift away, Jules nudged me. "Hey D, you still up?"

"Barely."

"I can't sleep."

I passed the joint over to her, but she waved it off. "That's not helping right now. It's making me more antsy."

"Really? I'm feeling spidery. Hey, that's cool we're both on the bug wavelength, which reminds me—"

"D, knock it off, I'm serious! I need to talk."

"Well I'm not stoppin' ya." I took another drag from the joint, giggling as I blew out the smoke.

"D, I mean it! I wanna talk to you about something."

"Uh oh, here comes the buzzkill! Make sure I don't overheat on the descent back to Earth, okay Jules?"

She snorted. "Forget it, D. I'll wait till you're sober."

"Come on Jules, don't be like that. I'm listening, I swear."

But I wasn't. I had already tuned her out. Kruder and Dorfmeister's beats rose up from the floor, intensifying the silence. Jules stared at me expectantly.

"Did you really mean it when you said you were in love with me?"

"Why would I lie to you about that?"

"I dunno. You been hung up on that Celeste girl forever, even before we became friends."

Images of her radiant face floated up like neon globs in a lava lamp. I tried to puncture them, but their membranes were impenetrable.

"I'm sorry, Jules. I know I haven't been fair to you. But you gotta understand, I've loved her since I was a kid, and that's hard to shake off, ya know? Besides, she's the only girl I ever proposed to."

"But she said no. Don't you think it's time to move on? Don't you think it's time to propose to somebody else?"

As she batted her eyes, I couldn't help laughing. "Are you serious?"

"Hell yeah! I wanna be your woman. Your one and only."

"You are Jules, you are."

"D, don't you dare try to play me. I know damn well I'm fightin' for space in that heart of yours. Why won't you let me kick her ass out?"

The words just slipped out before I could stop them. "Because I still love her."

Her smile vanished, a sneer taking its place.

"You got some fucking nerve coming in here, saying you love me, while you're still in love with somebody else." She snatched the joint from my hand, took a long drag, snuffed it out in the ashtray. "Were you thinking about her while we made love?"

"No Jules, I swear. I was too high to think of anything!"

"This ain't funny, D. How can you love two women at the same time?"

"It's possible, you know."

"D, you're trippin'. No fucking way."

"But I meant what I said. I love you."

She sighed. "The point is, I shouldn't have to compete with a ghost from the past. It just ain't fair." She crossed her arms in defiant punctuation, rolled away from me. "You need to leave."

I tried to flip her over, but she wouldn't budge. "Jules, come on . . . don't be like this. I wanna be with you. I already told you that."

She sniffed back some tears. "I can't keep doing this. I don't wanna be your fuck buddy anymore. I deserve better than that."

I remained quiet. I knew she was right.

When she finally turned around, all I could do was stare into her bloodshot eyes. "Let me ask you something. Is it just sex to you, or does it actually mean something?"

"It's fucking hot, if that's what you mean."

She rolled her eyes, making a thick sound in the back of her throat, like she was ready to spit venom at me. "That's what I thought. Get out."

Shooting out of bed like a projectile, she flew toward the bathroom. Somehow, I was able to intercept her.

"Wait Jules, I do feel a connection when we make love, I swear!"

She threw my hands off her hips, pushed me away. "Forget it, D. Just go."

"But Jules, let's talk about this. We can work through it."

Her gaze was more intense than I could bear. "I'm not workin' through anything until you nix that fucking bitch. You hear me?"

"There's no need to be mean, Jules, I mean, she's still—"

"SEE! You're still defending her, like she's still your girlfriend! Un-fucking-believable! I don't know what I was thinking."

Before I could stop her this time, she ran into the bathroom, locked the door, rattled the knob.

"Please Jules, don't let it end like this."

Even with the barrier between us, I could still hear her crying. "Too fucking late, D. You had your chance."

"But Jules—"

"GET THE FUCK OUTTA HERE!"

I recoiled from the door, knowing this was it. We were done. The truth was out in the open now, and I couldn't take it back.

Good riddance, I raged. She was just a placeholder for the real thing anyway.

Besides, I still had a four-hour drive to my weekend DJ gig at Trinity Nightclub in Seattle, and better yet, my other raver girl would be there, waiting for me. It was going to be another epic night.

Ω

Serotonin surged through my synapses, and as DJ Icarus, I was lost in the vortex of music again, like a mad scientist performing his sick sonic experiments.

Trance Tuesday midnight revelers packed the Blue Room, my favorite place to play trance and chill music. It captured my cool, celestial mood perfectly: Eight planetary lights orbited around a disco-ball sun that projected stars and snowflakes all over the walls, looking like one of those blue Antarctic ice caves I'd seen in pictures. This place felt more like home than my own bedroom.

Dancers' bodies corkscrewed to the beat, their hands raised in the air, some with drinks, others with glowsticks. They moved like an undulating wave to the pulse of the music—Ecstasy dancers glided like liquid; coke and meth heads jumped and twitched frantically; acid-shroom freaks grooved slowly, their eyes opening and closing corollas, filtering sunlight from a different dimension; potheads bloomed as wallflowers, nodding their heads with slight smiles and slit eyes, lost in some inner bliss; booze bashers bounced sloppily, sometimes off the beat, but always with abandon.

Welcome to the freakshow!

The crowd screamed at a fevered pitch while I torqued the EQ to a killer transition, chills pouring through my body like a shower of sparks. The dancers closest to the booth were smiling and wooing, enjoying the aural pleasure of the moment as well. Just as I dropped Armin van Buuren's "Shivers," the crowd cheered, clapped to the beat, sang along, and I was transported to that magical world. Again.

Ω

Celeste squeezes my hand, leans in. "You still with me?"

I smile back. "Always."

Cascada's "Everytime We Touch" blares like a siren, Celeste's face lighting up. "I love this song! Let's dance!" she squeals.

She drags me to the center of the dance floor, beaming. My heart racing, I grab her hips, pull her toward me, then kiss her tenderly, passionately. She holds my face like dove wings, and I fly into her embrace.

This hyperspace feeling washes over me as the room melts around us, funneling into our mouths, filling us up with light and sound.

Ω

Tweaking on a chemical peak, I finessed Paul Van Dyk's "We Are Alive" into the mix, watching music and color commingle. Neon green lasers fanned through the crowd, held in suspended animation by the thick smoke from the fog machine, while the disco ball radiated diamonds on the ceiling, walls, and floor. In the flash of the strobe lights, dancers appeared to pulse in slow motion, caught in the spell of some berserk photographer. LED beams radiated into the crowd, turning faces into prisms, eyes into sunrises. We rose up together.

I reveled in this deep connection with the audience; it was my only substitute for Celeste. As I slid the crossfader over, this hopeless place transformed into a palace. We coalesced, then ascended in love.

Ω

Back in Trinity's Main Room, my DJ shift over, I was tripping, soaring through my mental sky, being lifted higher and higher, beyond the clouds. The room expanded like a fledgling universe, nebular colors dancing in my eyes, blooming as kaleidoscopic stars.

Then, flashing out of nowhere, a mysterious woman appeared. In front of her face she held a Mardi Gras mask shaped like an infinity symbol, the black holes of her eyes siphoning light.

"Lower your mask," I said. "I want to know who you are."

"Don't you know who I am?"

"I don't know. Celeste, maybe?"

"Silly boy. Maybe a riddle will clear things up. Whose love for you knows no conditions, no bounds?"

"Um," I stammered, "sorry, these shrooms are really fucking with my head. I'm having a hard time thinking straight right now."

"Well, maybe if you thought more like a circle instead of a line, you'd figure it out."

"Can't you just tell me?"

"Now what fun would that be? It's not a riddle anymore if I give you the answer."

"Can you move your mask just a bit, so I can guess?"

"Well . . . I suppose a little hint wouldn't hurt."

She pinwheeled her mask—just for a second, just for a tease.

"I can't tell. It's like looking at two sides of a coin sideways."

"Sounds like you've stumbled upon a new paradigm!"

"Ha!" I shouted, more than laughed. The DJ's trance cycloned around us, Adam Lambert's "Ghost Town" spiraling out of its eye.

"What's so funny?" she asked playfully.

"I think I just got the joke."

"See, I knew it wouldn't take you long. Maybe this kiss will seal the deal."

Her kiss yielded never-ending strawberry fields seeping into my taste buds, secreting summer sun and sweetness. As she pulled her mouth away, our tongues stretched like saltwater taffy.

Then her identity hit me, like a bursting dam.

"Oh my God. I know who you are now."

"See, that wasn't so hard, now was it?" She transferred the mask to my face, and I could barely see her. "Who else can kiss you like this? It's like swimming in fucking ecstasy."

I dove into her mouth—descending fast and drowning—as electric champagne poured into my head with a bubbling bends.

I never wanted to surface.

Ω

I eventually surfaced onto a waterbed, a naked woman underneath me, touching me all over. Even in my altered state, I knew those graceful hands, that sexy skin, that irresistible desire pulsing between us. Her mask was propped up against the wall, staring right through me.

Marina sprinkled some white powder in a line from her navel to her mouth, and I snorted it from her belly to her breasts, then licked it all the way up to her lips. Before I kissed her, I paused: *Who is this goddess before me?*

The cocaine ignited another wave from the magic mushrooms, blasting my third eye wide open.

This golden aura surrounded her face, and I couldn't stop staring at her raven-black hair, her icy blue eyes sparkling like sunlight on the sea. She looked even more radiant than Celeste.

I froze, too afraid I'd desecrate this divine being, this Holy Moment.

"What are you waiting for?" she implored. "Kiss me already."

She reached up, pulled me underwater with her. Her lips were soft, wet, electric. No one kissed like Marina.

Not Jules. Not even Celeste. No one fucked like her either.

"I want you, D," she said breathlessly. "God, I've never wanted anyone so bad in all my life."

And I needed her, desperately. I couldn't wait to SHINE in SHE again.

When I finally slid inside her, we gasped in unison.

My God, I'm drowning. I can't breathe.

Enigma's "Principles of Lust" bubbled up from the depths of her stereo. The strong beat, the Gregorian chants, the woman's whispering voice, all carried me away in their powerful current.

Now, all I could perceive was this temple of Marina's flesh, where the sacred and the profane had merged, flowing together as one body of water.

I was floating, then sinking, descending deep into the ocean. And I never wanted to come up for air.

Ω

I woke up gasping for air. Once again, I had that recurring Celeste nightmare; only in this version, Marina had wrapped chains around my legs, pulling me down, deeper into the ocean. We drowned together.

In the silent darkness, I thought I'd died from my dream, but when I placed my hand over my chest to feel my rising breath, my beating heart, I realized I was still alive. Somehow, I hadn't killed myself. ~~Yet.~~ *Not yet, at least.*

As I tried to get my bearings, I felt the undulations of a familiar waterbed. *Oh thank God.* Fortunately, I hadn't wandered off anywhere else in my fucked-up state, and better yet, I'd managed to stay anchored to Marina at her Edgewood Park apartment in Bellevue, where I always crashed after my DJ gigs. The heat from her body, along with her light snoring, comforted me deeply.

Marina was on my left, her legs entwined with mine, her head resting in the groove of my arm, her long onyx hair covering most of her face, which had already lost its glow. While I stroked her hair, I thought about the way her arctic eyes had looked at me during sex. It had been such a strange look, one that had caught me off guard.

Underneath her coke-lust gaze was a profound sorrow, just like the sorrow that had haunted me for as long as I could remember. It was the pain of losing Celeste—over and over again—as a child, as a teenager, and most heartbreaking of all, as an adult. And now that pain was rising up, forcing me to face it—in all of its full-on ugliness—as if for the first time.

I wondered, was Marina now grieving the loss of me? Had I missed all the signs of our romantic connection, because I'd been too blinded by Celeste? Now, as I looked back at our times together, it was hitting me—with an increasingly sinking feeling—that all the signs had been there, unmistakably. Marina had loved me, and in return, I'd just thrown it right back in her face, only acknowledging the lust between us. Yes, it was clear now. I'd used her just like I'd used Jules. I suddenly felt sick.

Normally, Marina was such an intense, uninhibited lover, even when she wasn't high on drugs. Not even Jules and Celeste put together could rival her passion.

But tonight was different. After her initial wave of desire for me had subsided, it was quickly replaced by something darker, something much more disturbing.

Was it rage? Disgust? A fierce indifference?

I couldn't quite put my finger on it. All I knew was that tonight, once the drugs had worn off, she just seemed to be going through the motions, like she was playing a tiresome role she no longer wanted to perform. Like she'd rather be anywhere else—*with anyone else*—but right here with me.

Talk about a buzzkill.

Dear God, had I finally broken Marina? And Jules too? What kind of monster had I become?

The answer was obvious—the kind no woman in her right mind wanted to be with. I had become reckless. Callous. Despicable, even. And all because I'd closed my heart to every woman except Celeste.

This sick cycle had to stop, but I couldn't see any way out of it. It seemed I was trapped, unable to save myself. Maybe a smoke would clear my head.

Sitting bolt upright, I glanced at the clock. It was 5:55 a.m., and my insomnia had returned with a vengeance. It opened up a black hole inside me, its gravity well pulling me beyond the event horizon, until I could no longer resist. Until I had finally passed the point of no return.

Maybe I wasn't as sober as I thought. Maybe I was still in the grip of a sinister trip.

I have to get out of this room! I'll die if I don't!

Extricating myself from Marina, I jumped out of bed, threw on my *Dark Side of the Moon* pajamas, and grabbed the last joint from her nightstand. I opened the sliding door as quietly as I could, snuck out to the covered patio deck.

From the balcony, I lit up my joint, inhaled a long drag, blew the smoke out into the humid air. As I watched the wind drive a misty rain, streetlights glowed with a sentient white aura, humming to life before my eyes. Lyrics from U2's "I Still Haven't Found What I'm Looking For" condensed on my brain's dendrite leaves, soaking all my synapses with thoughts of Celeste.

I realized, with a peal of sardonic laughter, that my life was a joke. All the sex and chemicals in the world couldn't drown out her memory. She was the real drug I was addicted to—stimulant, depressant, hallucinogen—all rolled into one mind-bending joint.

Her glacier-blue eyes chilled the air around me. Her ghost was all I had left.

She fluttered through the street like a disembodied heartbeat, like a pulse stuck in a slow-motion strobe light.

Shit, I gotta start smoking lower-grade weed.

She passed by again, more slowly this time, levitating, her eyes burning into me, as a man chased her with a sword shaped like an upside-down rose. He was gaining on her fast. In a gravelly voice, he howled, "This time, I'm going to kill you for good!"

I tried to puff away the images, but my third eye was a movie projector I couldn't shut off. When the mysterious man finally caught up to her, he sliced her head off, and it just floated in the air like a helium balloon, right into the man's gaping maw. Then he morphed into an owl, screeching telepathically, *You're next.*

Oh God, help me!

But there wasn't a soul who could save me now. Before I could run, or even scream, the man siphoned my body into his mouth, swallowing it whole, condemning me to darkness.

Ω

I find myself trekking through a dark forest, pines framed with fresh snow, arctic winds blowing through my matted fur. The moon molts toward full, aurora shimmering in my eyes, simmering in my lupine brain.

But it is not a wolf moon tonight. The scent of owl taints the pure smell of winter, caution extending my nerve endings into the brittle air. I want to retreat, yet something inextricable draws me closer.

When I arrive at the only deciduous tree in the forest, I know why I'm here. In a large oak, now stripped bare, lurk three owls. The ferocity of their yellow eyes slows my heart to a crawl.

I know they've been waiting for me.

A trap made of frozen bone snaps out like a predator's jaw, ripping into my hind legs. I yelp, trying to break free, but the cold has turned the trap to steel.

They have me at last.

As two of them slice the air to attack, the other one's eyes bore into me. Instead of joining the fight, she stays back, birthing adult owls. Each new owl condenses from the spirit world, their feathers rippling in obsidian waves.

They soon become indistinguishable from the night.

Emerging at a rate of six per second, an auditorium of owls soon surrounds me, screeching, converging on my helpless body.

The fetid smell of carnage fills the air. In no time they're stabbing me with their beaks, blood erupting from me like small volcanoes. They remove my eyes with surgical precision. As they pierce my heart, I attempt to leap into the release of spirit.

But even that part of me doesn't escape. The female swallows it whole, birthing it into owl form.

I am lost, forever destined to repeat this cycle.

Ω

Little did I know, that vicious cycle was about to come to a screeching halt.

When I woke up later that morning, Marina was already gone. She usually left notes everywhere, leading me on an erotic scavenger hunt, but after a quick search of her apartment, I found nothing.

But wait.

There was a note perched on the coffee table, right next to her couch where we'd first made love. How had I not noticed it before? As I reached over to grab it, my stomach performed acidic gymnastics upon seeing Marina's big, loopy handwriting. I read it slowly, my heart pounding.

Dear DJ Dumbass,

Hey, guess what? The gig's up. The show's over. We're done.

Uh oh. I wasn't expecting this at all. I felt sick again, her words like cannonballs firing into my gut.

I just talked to Jules on the phone early this morning, and she told me you guys just broke up yesterday. Hmm, isn't that interesting? As I recall, you told me you two broke up several months ago. You're such a liar. And you think you're such a player, but you're just a pig like all the other pricks out there.

Oh shit. My lies had finally caught up to me. My Day of Reckoning had officially arrived. Truth be told, I was surprised it hadn't happened sooner.

And while I can easily stand the thought of losing you, I can't stand the thought of losing a good friend. If I would've known you were still with Jules, I never would've done all that sick sex and drug stuff in the first place. I lost one of my best college friends because of you. It SO wasn't worth it.

But I guess I'm partly to blame too. I've been so caught up with my life here in Seattle that I haven't talked to her at all since our big Halloween party last year. Now, I wish I had. Then maybe all this shit wouldn't have blown up in our faces. As soon as I told her what's been going on, she told me she's moving as far away from us as possible, and she's never going to talk to either one of us again. We damaged her pretty good, didn't we, D?

And even worse, Jules is completely devastated. She could barely talk through her tears. You know, despite all your stupidity and your commitment phobia, she was still willing to put up with all your bullshit because she thought you were the One. Believe it or not, she was ready to marry you.

But not anymore. Congratulations, Asshole! The same pain Celeste gave you, you've now given to both of us. Maybe you should actually try to heal from the pain of losing her, instead of dragging us down with you.

Wow, I never thought about it like that. And as reluctant as I was to admit it, Marina's insights were right on target. Her words were now like hammers, pounding into my skull, giving me a rager of a headache.

And my heart's broken too. Dylan, don't you see? I was crazy about you. I loved you. I'd fallen in love with you a long time ago, and I was just waiting to see when you'd finally get the hint that I wanted to be your girl. Maybe even your wife. And I know you were in love with me too, but you were too scared to admit it, or you were too scared to admit you were more in love with Jules than with me. Or, more likely, you were just too focused on yourself and all your perverted urges.

Well, congratulations again, D! You've fucked everything up with Jules, and you've definitely fucked everything up with me. And you know what? You'll never get either of us back. EVER.

But I guess you don't really give a shit, do you? Because you're with the person you love most. Yourself.

Good riddance, you piece of shit! You'd better not be here when I get back. I never want to see your lying, cheating ass again.

Sarcastically yours,
Marina

Ouch. I just sat there, reading her note over and over again, getting more depressed with each read. Funny thing was, I wasn't angry at her at all, because she was absolutely right. She was finally calling me out on all my bullshit, and I deserved every scathing word.

But what did hurt was getting confirmation that she had indeed loved me. I didn't know if I could ever forgive myself for fucking things up with her. She could've been the next Celeste. Or better. But now, I'd never know.

Marina's words echoed in my head: *Congratulations, Asshole!*

Honestly, how long did I think I could keep this gravy train rolling before it derailed? Sooner or later, the secret was going to get out. And she was right. I'd been so stupid about everything.

As I continued to stew over this whole situation, an urgent thought popped in my head: What if Marina was telling the truth about Jules leaving town? Or was she just bluffing to get me all riled up? Only one way to find out.

I threw her note on the floor, jumped off the couch, grabbed my overnight bag, and flew out the door. I couldn't get back to Spokane fast enough.

Ω

As soon as I pulled into the parking lot at Julie's apartment, my heart sank. There was no sign of her alien-green Kia Soul anywhere, which was strange, because she normally had the day off on Tuesday. I prayed she'd just taken a drive to clear her head.

I ran to the front door and buzzed for her apartment, for what felt like a million times, but I never heard that familiar click. So I tried calling and texting her,

52

but she wasn't answering her phone either. More than likely, she'd turned it off.

Suddenly, I heard that familiar click, and for a moment, my heart leapt. But when I saw a man opening the door instead of her, my heart sank again. I'd seen this guy a few times around the building, but I had no idea who he was. He was dressed in a green button-down shirt, khakis, and brown dress shoes, like he was somebody important.

"Can I help you?" he asked, eyeing me suspiciously.

"Yeah, I'm looking for Julie Lewis. She lives here and I can't get a hold of her."

His eyes narrowed. "She doesn't live here anymore. She moved out in a hurry and gave me the key before I could really talk to her."

"And how would you know that?"

"I'm the building manager. I've actually talked to Julie a few times. Are you Dylan?"

Oh God, did Jules talk to him about me too? I tensed immediately. "Yeah. Did she say where she went?"

"Nope. And if she had, I wouldn't be telling you. What did you do to her, man?"

"You wouldn't wanna know."

I turned around, practically sprinting toward my car. For a moment, I thought he might try to follow me, but when I looked back, he was already gone. I prayed he wasn't going to call the cops. But who could blame him? I probably looked deranged.

Dear God, it was déjà vu all over again. This whole scene reminded me of going out to Pittsburgh thirteen years ago to visit Celeste, only to find out that she and her dad had already moved out. Vanished without a trace. And just like Celeste, I had no idea where Jules had gone. And I'd probably never find out.

I was finally realizing I was the common denominator in driving all these women far, far away. But since I couldn't bear the thought of facing that truth right now, I raced home to do what I did best—escape by getting high. And this time, I might never come back down to Earth.

Ω

I was tripping full on to Pink Floyd's *The Wall*, "Comfortably Numb" blaring throughout my apartment. My bedroom expanded and contracted with my breath, and I could manipulate the space at will.

I felt powerful. I felt free.

But I was nearing the edge. This blotter was really potent—each wave of acid kept getting stronger and stronger. I didn't know how much longer I could hold on *before* ~~without~~ succumbing to oblivion.

White diamonds flashed above my head, while darkness kept encroaching, compacting. Perhaps after all that had gone on lately, tripping was a bad idea.

I kept breathing deeply, trying to let go with each increase in intensity, yet I couldn't stop my pounding heart, my rising body temperature. On one level I knew this was all in my head; on another, I knew it was all too real.

A pair of hands clawed through the darkness, blasting open a previously invisible curtain, revealing the crimson outline of a body, like the chalk drawing of a murder victim. The man who emerged spoke in the same timbre as Pink Floyd's lead singer David Gilmour, as if he were just another part of the song. "Man, you gotta lay off them drugs. They're killin' ya."

I had seen apparitions before while tripping, but never like this. This one actually seemed *real*. "Who the hell are you?"

"My name don't matter right now. What matters is you. You can't keep goin' on like this."

I chuckled. "And who are you? My fucking mother?"

"This isn't a joke, Dylan. This is a slow—well, maybe fast—suicide, if you keep goin' the way you're goin'."

"Hey man, how'd you know my name?"

"You gotta start being honest with yourself. The only reason you're actin' like this is 'cause Celeste rejected you."

"No shit, shadow man. Tell me something I don't know."

His form grew larger, the red outline superimposed over me now. "There are only three destinations for behavior like yours—jail, the hospital, or the graveyard. Not exactly a very promising future, now is it?"

"Again, tell me something I don't know."

His yellow owl-like eyes brightened, illuminating the room, yet further defining his shadow. "You need to turn your life around, or else you won't see Celeste again."

I sniggered. "News flash, shadow man, I'm never gonna see her again anyway."

His voice finally softened. "But you'd like to, wouldn't ya?"

"Well, of course, but I can't see how the two things are related."

Now it was his turn to laugh—well, guffaw, really. "The Lord works in mysterious ways, my friend."

"I guess, but what if I don't believe in God, huh? What then?"

"By the end of this adventure, you will, my man, you will." His smile glowed like a mouthful of fireflies.

"What adventure are you talking about, man? This is it. Life sucks."

"Ha! You're so cynical! Here, let me give you a glimpse."

Once the lights went out, all I could do was stare into the black. The air felt chilled and musty, like being trapped inside a cave. Mystery man's voice resonated in the fluctuating space. "Welcome to your own personal hell."

"I can't even see it, man. How bad can it be?"

"Look again."

A subtle lighting flickered as a movie screen rolled down. "Oh cool, so we're gonna have a movie night? What're we watching?"

"The Persistence of Celeste's Ghost."

Before I could stop him, or even say anything, his eyes turned into projectors, showing scenes of every second I'd spent with Celeste—when we were kids talking about dreams, when we were teenagers dancing and singing together, when we were adults making love, becoming one. The most intense scene was her rejection of my marriage proposal, stuck on a sickening cycle of repetition.

"Please tell me this is some kind of joke."

"No dice, man. This film is on infinite loop. It never ends, or moves on to new material."

"What? That's sadistic. Why are you torturing me like this?"

"Nah man, it's not sadism. It's masochism."

The music shifted to "Waiting for the Worms," as thousands of tiny worms bored into my pores, crawled into my cells, eating them from the inside out. I wanted to rip my skin off. "Why would I do this to myself? That doesn't make any sense."

56

"Of course not. Self-condemnation is the most illogical premise in the universe."

"But what did I do to deserve this?"

My question hung in the air for a moment, until the words got sucked into a vortex expanding below me. It wasn't long before I was swallowed up with them.

Ω

Darkness stretched out in front of me, portals in an infinite hallway glowing, brightening. The wind of an invisible presence hurtled toward me.

A man dressed as a medieval monk flashed out of nowhere. He kissed the large diamond cross hanging from his necklace, its facets blinding me. "I'd start praying now if I were you."

"Why? Am I in trouble?"

"No. But you're about to face the biggest test of your life. You think you're ready?"

"Do I even have a choice?"

He howled with laughter. Thousands of doors popped into existence like a string of firecrackers. He continued to stare at me.

"Holy shit, which door do I choose?"

He mirrored my serious expression, trying not to laugh. "These doors lead to anywhere you want to go. You can go to the past or future, but remember, time has no meaning here. In this place, the past, present, and future are one simultaneous, sequential moment."

"I don't understand."

"Someday you will. Right now, you're being strangled by the hands of clock time."

"That's rather gruesome."

"Hey man, sometimes the truth *is* gruesome!" He slapped me hard on the back, his laughter echoing down the never-ending hallway. After he ripped off his necklace, links showered down on the floor, melting into the carpet.

"Here, take this," he said, offering me his crucifix. The name Jeremiah Bolt was engraved on it.

"No man, I couldn't."

His glare ignited my eyeballs like gasoline. "I insist, man. It's a talisman. It'll protect you."

He pushed the cross into my chest, branding me with its heat. The electric shock funneled in two directions—one pooling in my heart, the other concentrating in my third eye—transforming my spirit into a powerful magnet. I was burning, my heart hammering, beams of light shooting out of every pore.

"Jesus Christ. I feel like I'm dying."

"Trust me, my brother, only what no longer serves you is dying. Just follow the intersection of your heartlight and headlight. It won't lead you astray."

A lightning bolt zapped one of the doors open in front of me. I squeezed the crucifix for good luck, said a silent prayer, then leapt toward the light.

As the light shifted to green, I realized I was totally unprepared for the new reality that awaited me, just on the other side of that threshold.

2

A LOVE LIKE LIGHTENING

Soft emerald light suffuses the air, as a tone starts low—slowly ascending—until the pitch becomes piercing. The sound forces me to stand, electromagnetic waves washing over me.

"Where the hell am I?"

No, my Son, you have not banished yourself there yet. You are still in Eden.

I gaze up at the shimmering aurora, the source of this familiar, yet mysterious voice.

"Then why isn't my heart beating? Why don't I feel alive yet?"

Don't worry, my Son, I have not diminished you; quite the contrary, I have augmented you. Look into the light and see!

A woman emerges from a magenta sun, bathing me in warmth. Ecstatic electricity sparks inside me—flowing up my legs, rising up my spine, fountaining out of my crown. Her smile is radiant.

"My God, did you put the sunrise in her smile? The nebulae from space in her eyes?"

She giggles, seeming infinitely young. "Well, we are descended from stars. That's how we got here."

"Wait . . . do I know you?"

"Of course. We were created for each other."

She holds out her arms, and my pulse kick-starts, accelerates. I approach cautiously. Flashes of light ignite in our hands—stars shooting off our fingers—choruses of chimes and angels singing for our celestial dance. We swing along a path of figure eights, gliding over a cosmic ocean.

I fall into her fluid flesh, splashing into her sapphire eyes; and on the tropical islands floating there, I taste the nectar of billions of flowers blooming, exploding into space. Our laughter binds our bodies into a tight atomic knot.

I have given you the power to create whatever your heart desires, and whatever you create, you will tend; and whatever you tend, you will love, just as I love both of you. Now, be as one mind, one heart, one spirit. Be as little children and rejoice, for the Kingdom of Heaven is your eternal playground!

She pushes me away for a second, just so I can feel the sting of separation. When she flees into the sky, I know exactly what to do.

Flying through the air, I sing to God in many octaves, a melody ancient, yet eternally new.

We soar into the Green Light together.

†

That benevolent light transported me three days later to Heartbreak Hill—that ill-fated spot where Celeste had rejected my marriage proposal. I just stood at the top of "The Hill," watching the crisscrossing traffic below, wondering what Bolt's Edenic vision meant for my life now.

Clearly, he had known Celeste would come back into my life somehow. If only I'd known that earlier, then I could've avoided most of the intense heartache over the last eight years. If only I'd known, as that Eden dream had shown me, that Celeste and I were created for each other, then I never would've lost faith in us. Then I never would've given up on life and spiraled into near self-destruction.

But now God had given me the green light, the go-ahead I'd been waiting for since our breakup. After nearly a decade, it was finally time to see my Celeste again.

I just couldn't believe this turn of events. It was more than I'd ever hoped for, even more than I'd dared to dream. I prayed I wouldn't suddenly wake up and come crashing back down into the nightmare of my old life.

As Max Graham's "So Caught Up" blared from the speakers of my wide-open car doors, I realized that for most of my life, I'd been so obsessively caught up in Celeste. Yet now, I was caught up in something else, something much more encouraging—an unexpected gift that had come wrapped in chrysalis. Listening to the song's lyrics, I imagined millions of monarchs launching into the air, filling the sky with their fluttering opal wings, then flying straight into my heart.

At long last, love was shining through the cracks of my concrete walls, all my internal prisons transforming into prisms. At long last, Heartbreak Hill had become Resurrection Ridge.

But what a long road to get here. I'd spent the last eight years returning to this spot on the anniversary of the Ultimate Rejection, sometimes even on half anniversaries, wondering why Celeste had refused to marry me. Even after rehashing that day—and every other day of our relationship—over and over again, I still was no closer to figuring out that mystery. It just didn't make any sense.

However, perhaps now the answers would finally reveal themselves. This time I'd come to Heartbreak Hill to leave behind my personal crucifixion from Bad Friday 2008, and instead usher in a much more welcome anniversary—March 25, 2016—as a true Good Friday, one that would hopefully lead to a powerful resurrection. My long winter hibernation was finally over, and now that spring was here, I could at last move from the Ultimate Rejection to the Ultimate Redemption. All thanks to this letter I held in my hands. This letter from Celeste. This letter that promised to change everything.

As I watched Celeste's letter flutter in the breeze, I wondered, why now? Why had she waited so long to contact me? Why even bother? I thought we were done.

Yet knowing Celeste, it was no surprise. It was just like her to cut me loose and leave me hanging—only to reel me in again—to the point where I was helpless to resist.

Our chase was back on.

The wind nudged the letter open, unfurling it in my hands automatically, as if under the spell of some invisible force. A crow cawed from atop a pine tree, then flew north in the direction of Celeste. Taking it as a sign, I slowly pulled the letter toward my eyes, my hands trembling.

Hi Dylie,

It's Celeste. Long time no see, right? I hope this letter reaches you. I only had your old address, and it was the only one I could find for you online. So if you're living somewhere else, I pray this letter somehow gets forwarded to you.

Well, lucky for you, I still live in the same apartment—that hallowed and haunted spot—where we once shared a blissful life, a life that had been cut too short, too soon. Even luckier for you, my masochistic inability to let go assured both of us I would receive your letter.

But unlucky for me, staying stuck in one place had been the only way to hold onto you. And even worse, you must've assumed I hadn't moved in all that time. Could I look any more pathetic?

Probably not. But at least you'd taken the time to search me out. At least you still seemed to care. That was something. Maybe there was still a glimmer of hope. Maybe someday, we could finally get back together, or at the very least, be friends. I'd take anything over this unbearable silence, this torturous distance between us.

I'm so sorry I haven't kept in touch like I promised I would, but it's all I can do to get even a few spare moments in the day. I'm busy working as a ski instructor and librarian, and when I'm not doing that, I'm taking online classes to get my master's degree in education. And then my two kids take up any free time I might have, but believe me, they're worth it!

And I'm sorry for not inviting you to the wedding, but I didn't want things to be awkward. Besides, I thought you might think it cruel of me, after what we've been through and all.

Yeah right, like I *ever* would've gone to a wedding that didn't showcase *us* as the happy couple. It would've been a huge slap in the face. We both knew I should've been the groom, I thought bitterly, as Billy Idol's "White Wedding" kicked up a blizzard in my head.

Anywho, I wanted to invite you up for Easter dinner with my husband Mike and my two kids, and maybe even an Easter egg hunt, if you're game. I live in Nelson, Canada (can you believe it?) and my address and cell number are below. You should be able to find it on your GPS. If not, call me.

Why in the world would she invite me up for dinner with her family? Maybe she was cruel after all, if she wanted to wave in my face what we almost had, but didn't. Still, I couldn't stop reading, her words seemingly composed of magnetic filings.

I know it's been a long time, and I know things didn't end well last time we were together. But I hope you've been able to forgive me. I've felt so bad over the last few years that I guess my guilt finally got the best of me. But you need to know something. I never meant to hurt you. I'm so sorry, Dylie. I know saying sorry doesn't make it right, but I don't know what else to do.

Well, I have an idea. You could divorce that loser Mike and marry me—*that* would make everything perfect. But Billy Idol was right: There *is* nothing fair in this world.

I pray this letter finds you well. And if you're married, bring your wife up. Or your girlfriend. I'd love to meet her. I'm sure she's beautiful. And I hope you're happy, Dylie. Of all the people I know, you deserve all the happiness in the world. I hope you know that.

Yeah right, *you* should be my wife. Then I'd be happy. Then all this misery never would've happened.

I couldn't help but laugh. Was Celeste serious? I would *never* bring any girlfriend—especially Jules—up to see her. Not after I'd let my obsession with Celeste sabotage my relationship with Jules. Not after I'd lied and cheated on her with ~~two of her best friends.~~ Marina And certainly not after all my antics had driven her out of my life for good. No, for now, I had to focus on healing my relationship with Celeste, whether that meant getting a second chance, or getting the closure I so desperately needed.

Please call or text me back. I want to know if you're coming up. I hope you do.

Love always,
Celeste.

My heart and throat caught on the words "Love always." Did she really mean them, or was she merely trying to be polite? Or even worse, was she trying to bait me again, exactly like she'd done ~~two~~ three times before? I just couldn't figure out her intentions, or why she'd even bother to send a letter after all this time.

Then it hit me.

This letter had to be the handiwork of Jeremiah Bolt, the apparent catalyst for this big turnaround in my life. It was the only explanation that rang true. The timing of Celeste's invitation was too perfect, too incredible, to be otherwise. My mind ignited with all the new possibilities, and a voice inside screamed, "THIS IS YOUR CHANCE! GO, GO, GO!"

Looking up at the cloudless sky, I laughed, in a way I hadn't laughed in a long time. Even if there wasn't a chance in hell of us ever being a couple again, at least I could finally see my Celeste. And get the reconciliation that was long overdue.

Already texting her, I smiled. Yes, Billy Idol was right once more: It was the perfect day to start again.

†

On the next day, the Saturday before Easter, I was hurtling toward Celeste's house, staring at the infinite blue in front of me, the sun quickly descending. As its rays shone through my Saturn Sky—which was ruby-red in honor of her birthstone—I smiled.

My prayers had finally been answered. At long last, I was going to see my Celeste.

I slid Sting's *Sacred Love* into the CD player and cranked up the volume, reminiscing about the times Celeste and I had spent during that Invincible Summer back in 2007, when we drove from place to place in Washington state, each one more exotic and promising than the last. The first track, "Inside," began with an ethereal sound, almost like a faraway train, then a whisper emerged, building in intensity toward a guitar and sitar melodic dialogue.

As Sting sang in somnolent tones, I wondered: *How long had my own heart been hibernating?*

For far too long. I prayed this trip would wake it up and bring it out into the sun. Once and for all.

I had Celeste's number ready to dial on my phone, but my nerves were getting the best of me. My heart hammered. I tried to catch my breath.

Here we go, I thought, a near decade of silence, finally about to be broken. Sting's voice softened to a murmur.

She picked up on the third ring. "Oh my God, Dylie, is that really you?"

I couldn't believe she still called me Dylie after all this time. "Yep, long time no hear, right?"

Her giggle sounded just like it always had. "So, you on your way up yet?"

"Yeah, I just left Spokane not too long ago, so I should be in Nelson in about three hours."

"Okay, well, be careful. It's starting to snow up here, and I don't know how much they're calling for."

"Okay, well, I'll try to take it easy, but it's hard not to put the pedal to the metal. I can't wait to see you again."

There was an awkward, pregnant silence, then just the sound of her breathing.

"Look, Dylie . . . I know things ended abruptly between us, but I thought we could still be friends."

My heart sank. I tried to focus on the road.

"Anyone coming up with you?"

"Nope, just me."

"Aw, that's too bad." She cleared her throat. "Anyway, I can't wait for you to meet my family, especially Elsie."

"Oh yeah? Who's that?"

"My daughter. She loves company, but she thinks Mom and Dad are *so* boring."

"And what about Mike? You're sure he's okay with this?"

"Yeah, he's fine with it, Dylan. Don't worry about him."

She paused again, this time so long I thought she'd hung up on me. "Celeste, you still there?"

"Yeah, sorry. I was just thinking."

My heart lifted, ever so slightly. "Oh yeah?"

"Well . . . on second thought . . . never mind. I'll just tell you when you get here."

"Come on Celeste, you know I hate surprises. Why can't you just tell me?"

"If I told you, it wouldn't be much of a surprise, now would it?"

"Come on, Celeste."

Another awkward silence.

"Well, all I'll say is, it's something that'll connect us for the rest of our lives."

What the hell? You gotta be shittin' me.

My heart jumped off a cliff, without a parachute. "Okay, well, I can't wait then."

"Cool, well, gotta go, Mike's coming in from chopping wood. I'll see you when you get here."

"Okay, great, looking forward to it."

"Oh, and Dylie?"

"Yeah?"

"I still care about you. No matter what, that'll never change."

And just like that, her gravity was pulling me—inexorably—toward her again. Singing along with Sting, I put my foot down on the accelerator and raced into the impending dusk, letting my past relationship with Celeste surge back to life.

†

While Celeste drives, dusk deepens around us.

Red at night, we're all right. Red by day, we're drifting away.

She plays David Gray's "This Year's Love" on her CD player, setting the mood perfectly, as always. Waves of chills wash over me, and it's all I can do to keep from crying. She catches my red eyes before I can hide them.

How does she see into me so well, like I'm transparent? She's always been able to peer into my soul, ever since we first met as kids. Even to this day, I've never been able to figure it out.

Now, the big question is burning in my dammed-up throat. "I just gotta know . . . do you love me?"

Her eyes always answer before her words. "Seriously?"

"I can't help it, Celeste. It's the question I've been chasing this whole time."

"Of course I love you. I told you that a long time ago." She looks away, stares down the road. "I just wish you could be me for a minute. Then you'd know, without a shadow of a doubt, how deep my feelings are for you."

I start thinking about what it would feel like to be her, and how it would feel to love me so passionately.

It's more than I can stand.

She smiles knowingly, squeezing my hand. "I've always loved you, Dylie. Ever since we were little kids. I just wish you'd trust our connection."

"I'm just afraid you're gonna leave again. You've done it before, you know."

"Well, I mean it this time. I'm not running away anymore."

"Then show me. I need to know you're gonna stay. I need to know you're gonna choose *me* over Mike."

Her eyes narrow as she grips the steering wheel tight. "Okay, fine. I'll show you how much you mean to me. But you have to promise *me* something too."

"Sure, anything."

"No holding back. It's all or nothing. I want you to give me everything you got."

She stares at me for a couple seconds. "Deal?"

"Sure, yeah. I can do that."

Once again tuning into the song, she says, "See, isn't this life sweeter when we're together?"

†

But clearly, this life wasn't sweet anymore. It was sour and bitter without Celeste. And now I wondered, could I follow up on that distant promise? Would I be able to free myself from our past and act like we'd never been in love?

I wasn't so sure. I wasn't even sure if this trip up to Nelson was a good idea.

Only one way to find out.

I got out of my car, stood staring at her. The waning full moon shone down on her like a surreal spotlight.

She looked different. Not as radiant. Muted, somehow.

With no more hesitation, she walked up to me, pulled me toward her, hugging me just like she used to do, all those years ago. I couldn't resist her gravity, and squeezed back. When she kissed me on the cheek, my face flushed.

There was that old spark again.

She let go. "I'm so glad to see you!"

Her sincerity shocked me. "Well, you know how I feel."

"Of course!" She flashed her trademark devilish smile—the one that melted me every time—and I couldn't stop the bodyquakes.

She must've thought I was cold, because she started rubbing my arms up and down, like a DJ scratching a record.

"Why don't you come inside, you know? Get warm."

Her words were echoes from eight years ago, reminding me of our first night making love, becoming One. If Celeste were toying with me, this was going to be a long, long trip.

I gulped, my pulse quickening. She led me inside.

†

As soon as we enter our new apartment as a couple, Celeste dodges several stacks of boxes on her way to her stereo, one of the few things we bothered to unpack.

Immediately she plays Loreena McKennitt's *The Mask and Mirror*, the defining album of our relationship.

To this day, I still can't listen to it. Too many reminders of what could have been.

"Why don't we get a bath and get cozy, make this place ours," she says, never taking her eyes off me. "Sound good?"

"I'd love to," I respond, stuttering a bit.

She kisses me softly, heads off to the bathroom. McKennitt's voice washes over me, the room rushing away in the powerful current of a past-life memory.

We glide through the crowd at the Marrakesh Market in Morocco, exotic meat smoke rising from the food stands, lanterns glowing like miniature yellow suns. The crescent moon smiles lopsidedly.

Finding a seam in the sea of bodies, we navigate the crowd, her rainbow skirt weaving between kiosks. She catches the eyes of a strange woman, right before we duck into her tent.

"Did you know her?" I ask.

She nods, lets the curtains fall behind her. As our breathing finally slows, we listen. All we hear are indistinct voices, horses' hooves, and the persistent percussion of street musicians.

"I think we're safe now," she says, her aquamarine eyes gleaming in the low light of the lamps.

The recognition of my *anam cara* is instantaneous. "Oh my God. It's you!"

"Yes, my love. I'm your beloved forever!"

The drumbeat outside invades the tent. As the beat grows louder and faster, all I'm aware of is the music, her jasmine perfume, the enigmatic terrain of her flesh.

"Dylan? You still out there?"

I blink several times, awakening from that distant, beautiful dream. "Yeah, I'm coming."

Entering the bathroom, I measure my steps. White candles on the perimeter of the bathtub cast her in an elegant, orange glow.

My God, has she set this all up, just for me?

"Come on in, the water's warm!" she says, beaming. "Ooh, and leave the door open. I wanna hear the music."

The water is almost too hot to bear, but I slide in behind her without complaint. I don't want to ruin this sacred moment.

"Soap me up. I want your hands all over me."

As soon as I rub shower gel on her graceful legs, it hits me. *Oh my God! It smells like jasmine.*

She turns, faces me, water splashing all around us. "I know, Dylie. You don't have to say anything."

Our skin melts, our bones fuse. Everything's in slow motion. Our mouths flow with an internal music, sweeping us away.

In between kisses, she whispers, "Welcome home."

†

The front door to Celeste and Michael's house creaked open, unveiling a gateway to a different, unwelcome dimension. For a moment, I thought about bolting, but when I realized this was my only chance to spend time with her, I steeled myself to stay.

The only comfort was the smell of peanut butter cookies infusing the house like perfume. It reminded me of warm Christmases at my grandmother's house.

Entering a small hallway, I noticed Celeste's living room directly on my left, with a teal couch and an oriental rug laid over a worn, hardwood floor. On the right was a room that looked part study, part bedroom. A dusty white shelf was cluttered with hardcover books, stacked and slanted, ready to avalanche. I wondered if I were sleeping in there tonight.

A boy, girl, and their father ran breathlessly into the hallway, laughing, as he said in a bad pirate voice, "Arrr, matees, it's off to the plank with ye!" The floorboards creaked from their heavy footsteps.

"Michael!" Celeste yelled. He stopped mid-stride, but the kids kept running away from him. "It's 9:30. The kids should be in bed by now."

"Well, they weren't tired yet, so I thought I'd wear 'em out first."

"You're the only one who looks worn out! Come over here and meet Dylan." Crossing her arms, she turned to whisper to me, "He's like an overgrown kid sometimes, I swear."

I smirked. Maybe I still had a shot.

Mike took a moment to catch his breath and wipe the sweat from his brow, then walked over to me. He was about six foot three with a reddish, unkempt beard, wearing a navy PITT Panthers T-shirt, grey sweatpants, and dirty white socks. As he slid across the floor, he extended his hand to me, displaying his prominent incisors. "Hi Dylan, I'm Mike."

He gave me a crushing grip, making a few of my knuckles crack. I tried to equal the strength of his handshake, but failed. "Hmm, awful soft hands for a man."

I glared at him. "What the hell is *that* supposed to mean?"

The two kids came running around again, and he quickly corralled them, almost clotheslining them to the floor. They continued to giggle. "Come on Daddy, keep pwaying with us. You can't just stop!" the boy whined.

"Hold on a sec, kids," Celeste said. "I'd like you to meet our guest, Dylan."

They looked up at me with curious expressions, the way cats might regard a stranger through a window. The girl's eyes were bright blue, the boy's dark brown. "This one here is Elysia." She stuck out her little hand.

The gesture was so cute, I had to smile. "Elysia, pleasure to meet you. That's a pretty name. I'm Dylan." I shook her slender hand, noticing the purple polish on her fingernails with little red and green flowers painted on them. She kept staring at me, and I couldn't stop looking at her nails. Those flowers seemed significant, symbolic somehow.

"And this is Luke," Mike said, waving his hand to point at his son, his voice full of pride.

Luke was chunkier than Elsie, but no more than six inches shorter, wearing brown corduroy pants and a yellow Sponge Bob T-shirt. I tried not to laugh at his raccoon eyes and corkscrewed brown hair. He put his hand up for a high five, and when he smiled, I noticed he was missing both of his front teeth.

I slapped his raised hand. "Yeah, my man!"

"You-ah not my man, Daddy is," Luke said, hugging Mike's tree-trunk legs.

"Everyone calls me Elsie, but you can be my man anytime, Dylie, I don't mind." She giggled, a little too much like Celeste. "Can I hug you?"

I glanced at Celeste and Mike, and they nodded, but only Celeste was smiling. "Sure."

She ran up to hug me. Her blonde curls brushed up against my jeans, the heat of her body radiating up my leg. Her gaze was unshakeable. In her face I saw Celeste's features—slender nose, angular face, cute ears, thin lips. But there was something else, something eerily familiar about the shape and color of her eyes.

"Mike, we gotta get these kids to bed," Celeste scolded. "We've got a long day tomorrow."

"Sure thing, honey." He walked over to give Celeste a kiss, longer than what was comfortable for me—or the kids—then shook my hand even harder than the first time. I swore he was trying to break a finger or two.

"Come on kids, let's go up to bed for story time!" As he chased them up the stairs, they giggled and screamed all the way up, the door slamming shut behind them.

I looked at Celeste. "I see what you mean."

She rolled her eyes, nodded. "Told you he was a big kid. So, are you hungry? I have some peanut butter cookies, if you want."

"Sure, they smell delicious."

She led me over to the study I'd seen earlier. I laughed when my earlier suspicions had proven correct. "So, this is your room. I apologize for the mess, but your bed's made, and the room's clean otherwise."

"Well, at least there's plenty of reading material!"

She chuckled, squeezing my arm affectionately. "Go ahead and make yourself at home. I'll get you a couple cookies and some milk."

I stepped cautiously into the room, rolling my suitcase next to the bed. On the comforter was a mandorla—in the left circle whirled a powerful hurricane, in the right swirled the Milky Way, and at the intersection stared a large eye with an indigo iris.

Following the eye's gaze up to the commotion above, I heard Mike's baritone, then sometimes falsetto voice, while he read his kids a bedtime story. I couldn't make out any words, but there was something soothing about the rise and fall of his voice. It made me want to be a father.

"Here ya go, Dylie," Celeste said, breaking my trance. She handed me a white paper plate with three cookies and a glass of milk.

I still couldn't believe she called me Dylie after all this time. I put the plate and glass on the oak nightstand next to the bed. Before she turned around, I said, "Celeste, wait."

I tried to read her expression, but couldn't. There was a time when I could read every nuance, every pore on her face.

"Sure, what is it, Dylie?"

I paused, looking down at the mandorla for courage. "I know you're married and all, but, I just gotta know. Do you still love me?"

Her smile surprised me. "Of course I still care about you. But we can talk more about that later. Besides, I have a big surprise for you."

My heart caught in my throat. "Come on, Celeste, quit teasing me. What is it?"

"You'll see."

She winked, kissed me on the cheek, said goodnight, and closed the door behind her. I stood there, staring at the door for several minutes, rubbing the spot where her wet lips had just touched.

Unfortunately for me, the magic was still there.

†

The streetlights outside the garden glow magically as we follow a stone path to the center of a bridge. Huddling together, Celeste and I look down at the somewhat opaque water, dark algae floating in the pond. We watch koi swimming back and forth, their colors muted. I imagine we've stolen their colors, rainbows rippling around our bodies.

"Wow, it's really beautiful out here." My voice seems unusually loud in the silence.

"That's why I like to come up here. It's so peaceful."

I slide my hands down to her buttocks, squeezing their firmness, and she moans, driving me to kiss her harder. I just want to kiss her forever, her lips an exotic nectar from a long-ago, forgotten paradise.

Caressing her face, I say, "You're amazing, you know that?"

She smiles, leads me to a wooden bench. A waxing half-moon brightens the night sky, a few pale stars tethered to its pendulum.

Nocturnal music blooms, settles in my ears—distant cars whoosh down the road; crickets chirp and cicadas buzz from the trees; bull frogs bellow from the pond. Fireflies illuminate the Japanese garden with their dazzling, dancing lights, flashing in time with this symphony composed just for us.

Celeste reaches out for my hands. "Whatchu thinkin' about?"

"It feels like we're in the Garden of Eden right now. It feels like home."

"Now you see why this place is so sacred to me."

Leaning into my shoulder, like a natural groove just for her head, she puts her left arm around my upper back, her right hand on my thigh. "I could stay here forever," she says. "Couldn't you?"

"Absolutely." I rest my head against hers, close my eyes. As the tree frogs join the chorus, I realize I've never been in such a perfect moment.

"But you know Celeste, you have a way of making everything sacred."

"You're sweet, but it's not me. It's just that when we're together, everything becomes infused with the numinous."

I keep my eyes closed, not wanting to break this fragile spell she's cast on me. "Do you rehearse these things before you say them?"

She giggles. "I wish. You just inspire me, Dylie. You bring out my inner poet."

I stand up, take her hand. Our fingers interlock, forming a steeple of flesh and bone. We amble along the gravel path, listening closely to our next steps, our next breaths, as the night shimmers in silence.

†

That silence pierced me, woke me up in the middle of the night. I patted the bed for her, but all I felt was cold, empty space. I tried not to scream.

How would I find the courage to accept this new life with Celeste, but without her?

In my head, The Edge kept playing the outro of "With or Without You," over and over again, tormenting me.

I had lost paradise. There was no denying that now.

Only one question remained: *How could I get it back?*

The answers came not in words, but in a dream I would always remember. And in a memory I could never forget.

†

The Bangles' song "Eternal Flame" plays softly on a jukebox while I watch Michael and Elysia dance together, yet never in sync. On a large white wall, a green starlight flashes over the name CHRIST written in black graffiti letters. Celeste shows me her wedding ring, but it isn't a diamond, or any gemstone at all. It's one of those ring pops. A resonant voice unfurls from its ruby facets: *God has given you the green light. Dance in your radiance!*

†

"No, keep the light on. I want to see you," Celeste insists before I can turn off my lamp. She grabs my hand, places it on her waist, and I rub her hipbones like stone talismans.

"I should probably get some protection."

"No." Her tone is emphatic. "I want to feel you the way it was meant to be."

We are engulfed within one another again, my breath momentarily drowning inside her. She pulls the covers—wave-like over us—as if this union were too sacred for anyone to witness. Even God.

I press into her as far as I can go. She arches her back, draws me in, our eyes locking in blue-sky fusion.

"I can't get close enough to you," she whispers, desperation clawing at her voice.

She wraps her legs around me, pressing us hermetically together, curling her fingers, willow-like, around my face. As we kiss, our eyes remain open, afraid we might sever our connection if we close them. In the ocean of her flesh, our blood surges and crests, converging and rippling in seismic orgasms, until we crumble under the oxytocin waves demolishing—ever so gently—the shores of our separation.

†

Celeste and I were forever separated. That was the reality now, and I just couldn't face it.

A knock at the door startled me.

"It's me, Dylie," Celeste said. "You up yet?"

Every time she called me Dylie, it was a reminder of what we no longer had.

"Yep, just getting ready."

"Okay, well, you wanna come out and join us? I know Elsie's been dying to play with you all morning."

"Really?" I threw the covers off, sat up at attention. "Uh, sure, I'll be out in a minute."

"Great. If you need me, I'll be in the kitchen fixing dinner."

I walked up to the door, cognizant of the barrier between us. "Do you need any help?"

"You're sweet, but I think me and Mike can handle it. You just keep Elsie out of our hair for a little while."

"Okay, no problem."

There was a pause, then another rap at the door. "Can Dylie come out to play?"

I chuckled. Her voice was a perfect imitation of the Green Goblin from *Spiderman*.

"Sure Elsie, I'll be out in a sec." I put on my sneakers, checked my dark-circled eyes in the small mirror on the back of the door. Taking a deep breath, I opened the door to see Elsie's smiling face. Her blue dress reflected her big-sky eyes.

"Wanna play a game?" she asked, batting her eyelashes. As she gripped the game box, I noticed the red flowers on her fingernails were flaking off. I wondered if that meant anything.

"Sure, whatchu got there?"

"Hey, you look kinda sad. Something wrong?"

Her empathy caught me off guard. "Nah, I'm fine. But you're sweet to ask, though."

"I know. Wanna play Life?"

"You bet. They had a version of this game when I was growing up."

She looked down at the box, her mental gears grinding. "Wow, this game must be really, really old then."

I laughed at her unintentional wit. "I guess it is, but it's still fun. Let's play!"

We power-walked through the living room into the dining room. The walls were painted a soothing cornflower blue, and at the center of the tiled floor was an oblong dining room table with a white lace tablecloth. I was feeling déjà vu, like I'd walked into a room inside one of my dreams.

Elsie threw the game box lid at me, and I caught it just before it hit me in the head. All I could see was the word IF flashing out of LIFE.

In that moment, I knew. Elsie was up to something. Or maybe Jeremiah Bolt was conspiring with her. I swore I could feel his presence in the room.

She took out the plastic cars and pegs from a ripped Ziploc bag, then handed me a blue peg and a royal blue car.

"How'd you know that's my favorite color, Elsie?"

She smiled. "Cause it's mine too." She picked out a pink car and peg, placed both of our cars on the starting line. Pointing to the spinning wheel she said, "Your turn. Guests play first."

"Why thank you, Elsie, aren't you gracious?"

Again, I saw so much of Celeste in her face. But when I noticed something else familiar, my stomach jolted.

"If you don't go soon, I'm gonna take your turn."

"Okay, okay." I spun a three, but before I could even move my car, she leaned in, moved it for me. "Why thank you, Elsie."

"You won't be thanking me after I beat you."

I delighted in her competitive spirit. She spun a ten, then took the work route instead of the school path. "Don't you wanna go to college first?" I asked her.

"Nah, I wanna start making money right away. Mommy's still paying off her student loans."

"Hey, me too! But I can tell already, Elsie, you're smarter than the rest of us."

She smirked. "You bet!"

Staring at my car several spaces back, she said, "Do you mind if I spin for you? You'll have a fighting chance then."

I didn't even get a chance to answer. She twirled the wheel to a nine, dragged my car to a STOP space that read, "Return to real life. Get a job!" I rolled my eyes. The game board sounded like my parents.

"Uh oh Dylie, time to enter the real world!" She laughed, like she knew what that meant.

When she spun a four, she landed on the "Get Married" space. I wondered if she'd planned it that way. Winking, she put a blue peg next to her up front in the car, followed by a pink peg right behind them.

"Whoa, Elsie, don't you think you're jumping the gun? You just got married, and now you're having kids already?"

"Well, Mommy didn't wait, so why should I?"

I almost choked on the spit I was trying to swallow. "Wait . . . what?"

"Come on Dylie, do the math."

I stared at her, feeling this bizarre sensation that *she* was the adult, and *I* was the child. I couldn't shake it.

"Don't you see? It's you and Mommy up front, and me in the back. The way it's meant to be."

I just sat there, my mouth agape. Elsie was right. It *wasn't* meant to be this way. I wondered, if Celeste and I had done things differently, would Mike be the one visiting, and I the happy husband?

Damn. If only Celeste hadn't rejected my marriage proposal.

†

Celeste turns toward me, her feline face capturing me, drawing me into her blue eyes. In the dimming light, her features look elven, and I half-expect to see pointy ears sticking out of her blonde hair. I swear she's a divine being—too beautiful, too pure—to be loved by a mere mortal like me.

She kisses me softly, the curls of her hair tickling my cheek, bolstering me to make my big move. Time is closing in, constricting. Yet still, I wait. I don't want to rush the moment.

Putting her arm around me, she rests her head against mine, seemingly oblivious.

"Hey, I guess your dream did come true," I say, trying to stall. "Here we are in Washington."

"I told you it would. Our whole journey together has followed rivers, and we even went all the way to the ocean. You see, our connection is like water—fluid and everchanging."

I close my eyes to steady myself from the vertigo, and when I reopen them, Spokane crystallizes into my ~~radio~~ vision again, motionless. Red lights on ~~the cell phone~~ towers keep a regular rhythm, playing a silent musical composition, while a bright full moon shines through my ears, illuminating the cul-de-sacs of my brain, shouting, "Ask Celeste! Ask Celeste! Ask Celeste!" My heart beats triple time to the flashing towers, my throat tightening, running dry.

This is it. The inevitable moment. There's no turning back now.

Pulling her into my embrace, I kiss her passionately, and she moans. Her smile soon breaks our kiss. "What was *that* for?"

"It's how I feel about you, Celeste. I've never felt this way about anyone, and I want to feel this way with you forever."

I exhale sharply, get down on one shaky knee. When she realizes what I'm doing, her hands shoot up to cover her mouth. "Oh my God, Dylan!"

I struggle to speak. But then the words just surge, like rivers unleashed from their dams. "Celeste, I love you so much. I've found paradise with you, and I never want to let you go. I want to be with you forever. Will you marry me?"

Time seems to stop. Her eyes deepen, zoom closer, as if I'm observing a nebula through a telescope. I've never felt so connected, yet so distant, like having an out-of-body experience, or floating in deep space.

Finally, she speaks.

"Oh my God, Dylan! Are you serious?"

"Serious as a heart attack, which I'll have if you say no."

She pauses, biting her lip. "But we haven't even been together for a year yet."

"That's not how I see it. I've loved you since we were kids. You're my first and last love, you're my everything. I want a lifetime of these moments with you."

"But where's your ring?"

"Really? That's your response right now?"

"Dylie, I'm just joking. I don't care about a fucking ring."

"Then why bring it up in the first place?"

She shakes her head, lifts me up under my arms. "Come on, Dylie, get up. I wanna talk to you face to face."

As soon as she rubs my knuckles, I know where this is going. I rise slowly, hoping she'll change her mind before our eyes meet.

"Don't you love me?"

She recoils, her brow scrunching. "Of course. I'm crazy about you."

"And I'm crazy about you. What else matters?"

Her brows rise over her widening eyes. "It's not that simple, Dylan. We'd have to totally change our lives for this."

"So? I'm prepared to do that."

Her body suddenly goes limp, like all the air is being squeezed out of her. "But I'm not."

A thick silence hangs in the air. My heart leaps off the cliff, no parachute.

"Well, look. If it's too soon, I understand. We can always take a long engagement, like, four or five years. I mean, I'll do whatever it takes."

Her hands drop, but her gaze holds. "I know you would, Dylie. That's not the problem."

"Then what *is* the problem?"

"I already told you, I'm not ready for marriage. I wanna finish college, travel, and maybe go back to school. There's still a lot I wanna do before settling down."

"And you can do all that. With me. Like I said, we can do a long engagement, or do the long-distance thing for a while if we have to. We've done it before."

"You're not hearing me, Dylan. I don't *want* to do the distance thing again. I can't be constantly thinking of you from afar."

"Well, we only have one more year of school. And it's like you said, then we can start planning our lives together."

"But I don't want you to give up your life for me. I couldn't live with that guilt."

"I don't give a fuck about guilt. I want to build my life around you."

Her eyes sag, invisible sand bags dragging them down. "That's sweet, but I can't let you do that."

I can't hold back any longer. "This is about your goddamn freedom, isn't it? You don't want anyone or anything holding you back. Especially me!"

Her eyes soften, her hands reach out for me. She starts crying, then whispers into my ear. "I'm sorry, Dylie, but I just can't do it. I can't give you what you need right now. I'm just not ready."

I can already feel the current of sorrow pulling me under. "I'm never gonna give up on us."

"I know, Dylie. I know."

As she collapses into me, I squeeze her, never wanting to let go.

†

She emerged in the archway of the kitchen, watching us. I stared back, wondering where my Celeste had gone.

"Elsie, why don't you go into the kitchen and wash up. We'll be ready to eat soon."

"But me and Dylie were having fun playing games."

"You two can play more later. Right now, you need to wash your hands."

"But look Mommy, all three of us are driving through life together. Don't you wanna join us?"

Celeste scowled. "Elsie, just go get your brother and help set the table. Now."

"Aw come on, Mom, I wanna play—"

"Just do it, okay!"

Elsie mimicked her mother's expression, and I had to stifle a laugh. "Fine, Mom. But you know I'm gonna have to do all the work anyway. Luke never gets it right." She jumped off her chair, stormed into the kitchen.

Celeste's scowl deepened. "What the hell's going on here, Dylan?"

Whenever she dropped the "ie" and added the "an" to my name, I knew I was in for it. "We're just playing Life, Celeste. I mean, really, it's no big deal."

She kept standing, her arms crossed. "You know that's not what I'm talking about."

"Then you've lost me."

"I thought I made myself clear over the phone. I don't want to rehash the past."

"Believe me, you've made that *abundantly* clear."

"Then why are you putting ideas into Elsie's head?"

"Ideas? What fucking ideas?"

She looked down at the car with two pink pegs and a blue one. "That one," she said, pointing down at the white church.

check

I held up my hands like she was pointing a gun at me. "Hey, that was all Elsie's idea. I had nothing to do with it."

"Sure, blame the kid. Maybe Mike was right. Maybe it *was* a bad idea to invite you up here."

I glared at her. "This hasn't exactly been a pleasure cruise for me either, Celeste. Everything in this house reminds me of what I could've had with you. Is that why you invited me up here? To torture me? To rub it in my face?"

Her face looked pained as she came toward me, like she was walking on broken glass. "Come on Dylie, you know I'd never do that," she said, sitting down. "Not even if I was mad at you."

"Then why invite me up? What could possibly be the reason, huh? I'm *dying* to know."

She paused, glancing back into the kitchen. "Well, I guess I should tell you. No point waiting anymore, I guess."

"Hey everybody, who's ready for some divine swine?" Mike announced, carrying a tray with a big honey ham.

My glare turned to him. His smirk told me everything I needed to know.

Feels like déjà vu. This wasn't the first time Mike had interrupted an important moment with Celeste.

†

On our penultimate night together, our lovemaking is foreplay for spiritual connection.

"I feel like I'm melting into you," Celeste whispers, her words filling the space between us.

I pull her closer like a warmer, more welcoming skin.

Then, without warning or concern, the phone rips through the silence, a violence to this sacred moment.

"Just let it ring," I implore her.

"It might be an emergency." She sits up, reaches for the phone. "Hello?"

"Hey babe, it's me. You still up?"

I recoil. I know exactly who it is.

"Obviously."

"Is he still there?"

"Yeah I'm still here!" I announce.

She smacks my shoulder, her glare cutting through me. "Shhh!"

"What?"

"Aw baby, I can't believe you're living together already," he says, slurring his words.

"That's none of your business, Mike."

"Aw man, and you're sleeping with him already too? I can't take it."

"I'm sorry, Mike."

"Why baby? I still love you."

I want to rip the phone out of her hand, tell Mike to go to hell, and yank the phone cord out of the wall. But I restrain myself.

To this day, I still don't know why.

"Look, we can talk about this later. It's almost four in the morning, and I'm tired."

"But baby, you hardly know him. You and me, we got a history together, ya know?"

"I know, Mike."

She leans into her bent knees, gripping the phone with both hands. Her blonde hair looks brown in the dark.

It's like I'm not even there anymore.

"Look babe, I'm sorry for all the mean things I said. But I want you back. We belong together."

"It's too late, Mike. You know that."

"Please, baby. I'll do anything. I'll be the man you've always wanted."

"She already has the man she's always wanted."

She doesn't even turn around. "Was that him?"

"Never mind, Mike. Look, I gotta go. It's late."

"Just tell me this. Do you love him?"

"Good night, Mike."

After I stare at her back for a small eternity, she finally turns around. Even though her blue eyes say it, I still have to ask, just to hear her answer.

"Well, do you?"

She nods, reaching out for me as we embrace. Her heart hammers against my chest, her body quivering, her warm tears dripping onto my cheeks.

I sigh heavily. I know now.

There was absolutely nothing I could have done. Our demise was inevitable.

And there was nothing I could do now. All I could do was sit here and watch some other man be married to my soulmate, observe him raise the kids that should've been mine.

At the head of the table, Mike passed around the plate of ham, first to Luke, then Celeste, then Elsie, and finally, to me. Despite his air of nonchalance, I knew what he was up to. He wasn't fooling me.

I tried my best to ignore him, for Celeste and Elsie's sake. I took a bite of the ham, and it practically melted in my mouth—part sweet, part salty. "You weren't kidding about the ham," I said.

Mike laughed and grabbed his belly. "Hey man, I take my pig very seriously. Ham, pork, bacon, sausage—you name it—if it squeals, it's a meal!" He made oinking sounds as the kids laughed uproariously.

At least someone thought his antics were funny.

Celeste smacked his arm. "Mike, please, we have company."

"Well, somebody has to lighten the mood around here, jeez." He stared at me while the kids continued to giggle. I returned his gaze, flashing him a cocky grin.

Celeste rolled her eyes, shook her head, mouthed a silent apology to me. "Come on Mike, let's get the rest of this show on the road."

He passed the garlic and rosemary mashed potatoes, candied yams, fresh string beans, homemade bread, and fresh salad in short succession.

Celeste turned to Luke. "Why don't you say grace, honey, just like you always do?"

His brown eyes almost lightened to amber. "Okay," he said, nodding solemnly. As he bowed his head and folded his fingers together, I couldn't tell if he was praying seriously or mocking the process, but either way, I had to hold back a laugh.

"De-ah Wawd," he began, "pwease bwess us Wawd, and thank you for the good food and good company."

I caught him giving his sister a mischievous grin. He winked at me. "And wet me get the most candy today duwing our Eastah egg hunt."

"What!" Elsie cried. "That's not fair, Mom. Tell him it's not fair!"

Traces of a smile edged at the corners of Celeste's lips. "Come on, Luke, you know better. Pray for your sister too."

Elsie smiled defiantly. It was like looking at a mirror of myself.

"Okay Mommy, if you say so. And wet my sistah get a wot of eggs too. Amen."

"That was very sweet, Luke," I said. "One of the best prayers I've heard in a long time!"

His expression turned serious. "Didn't Mommy tewl you? I wanna be a ministah when I gwow up."

"Well, you certainly have the right name."

"You'll have to get rid of that Elmer Fudd accent first. No one'll be able to keep a straight face when you say, 'Deawy bewoved, we ah gathad he-ah today, in the pwesence of the Wawd . . .'" Elsie mimicked, giggling loudly.

"Elsie, that's not nice," Celeste reprimanded, trying to suppress her own laughter.

"I'm just saying what we're all thinking."

"That doesn't sound like an apology to me, young lady."

Elsie rolled her eyes, crossing her arms tightly as she stared at him. "Fine. I'm sorry, Luke."

"So Elsie," I said, trying to keep the peace, "what do *you* want to be when you grow up?"

"I'm gonna be a doctor." She glared at Luke. "I'm gonna help people *for real*."

"Wuke was a doctah in the Bible."

"I think you mean Luke, don't you? Say it with me, lllllllllll!"

Luke tried to match the sound, but couldn't. She took her tongue from its exaggerated L position and flicked it at her brother.

"Speaking of real jobs," Mike interjected, "what is it you do again, Dylan?"

ork ¹ (Immediately) I tensed like razor wire. Now the real Mike was coming out. "I thought Celeste told you. I'm a DJ."

"Yeah, but how do you make ends meet as a DJ? That doesn't sound like a very profitable or fulfilling career to me."

I swallowed hard, pushing down the rising acid in my gut. "What would you know about it, huh? Besides, I bet I make more money than you."

"I don't see how. I mean, I'm a general contractor. I make real good money *and* provide something people will always need—homes."

"And, people will *always* need music and wanna have a good time. Maybe if you got out more instead of being stuck at home all the time, you'd realize that."

Celeste's face reddened. The kids looked on, their eyes wide, their mouths hanging open. "That's enough you two. Let's just have a nice dinner."

"Look man, if you wanna go W2 to W2, let's do it," Mike said.

"As if I carry my tax paperwork with me at all times!" I chuckled.

Celeste wasn't laughing, spinning a string bean on the end of her fork.

He waved off my comment. "The point is, Dylan, I don't see how you could ever support a family as a DJ."

He said "DJ" like it was the lowest form of life on Earth.

"Even if you make enough money—which I highly doubt—that's still not a lifestyle for raising a family. I mean, all those late nights, more women and drugs than you know what to do with? That *can't* be good for any long-term relationship. Know what I mean?"

His smirk sickened me.

"Daddy, what ah dwugs?" Luke piped in.

Celeste glowered at him. "Watch what you say, Mike."

"Yeah, Daddy, you're being mean," Elsie threw in.

I just started at Mike, unable to believe he was coming at me like this. Hell, I didn't even like the guy, but at least I'd been willing to play nice. But not anymore.

"You don't know me. I can handle my life just fine. And besides, I don't play clubs or party anymore. That part of my life is over."

He raised his hands in the air. "All right, all right, Dylan, whatever you say. Look, all I'm sayin' is, it's not a job most of us *grownups* would do."

I was about to fire back, but Elsie's eyes entreated me not to.

Celeste squeezed my leg under the table without looking at me. If there were ever an opening to exploit, it was now.

†

Striding into our old apartment's kitchen—after our first night sleeping together—I find Celeste wearing my shirt and her teal panties, nothing else. Light from the patio window streams in, highlighting light blonde hairs on the back of her legs. I just stand there, admiring her beauty, but she doesn't see me yet. She's too busy unpacking plates from boxes and stacking them in the upper cabinets.

"Hey babe, whatchu up to?"

The plates shake in her hand, but before she can drop them, she gracefully sets them up in front of our chairs at a small dining table, where silverware and glasses of orange juice have already been set up.

"Jesus, Dylan, you scared me!"

"Well, you know, I have been working on my ninja skills!"

She giggles. "C'mere, you!"

I bearhug her, pick her up, twirl her around the kitchen. Her hair flows down to my shoulders, and I smell my own cologne on my shirt collar. She kisses my neck.

She embraces me like no one else, her hugs more intimate than sex.

As she runs her pinky fingers down my chest, I shudder, marveling at the raw power of our connection.

"Ooh, you're getting me all hot again," she says, pulling away. "We can continue this later. Right now, I wanna make these pancakes for you."

"They smell great. You want some help?"

She stares at my bare arms, chest, and stomach. "Not at all. You just sit down at that table and look pretty. That's all _you_ need to do."

I kiss her cheek, sit down at the kitchen table. Another sacred silence falls over the room, and I am overcome by this simple act of domesticity. This single moment of perfection.

The radio plays Sting's "Sacred Love" as Celeste sings along perfectly in tune. "This song makes me think of you," she says. "It seems like it was written just for us."

"Well, it should be our song then, right?"

Her smile is more than I can bear.

"Absolutely! I can't think of anything more sacred than our connection." Her gaze intensifies. "We're like Adam and Eve, you know? We were made for each other, and every time we're together, it's like the Garden of Eden."

My God. Could this be real?

Celeste sets a plateful of pancakes on the kitchen table, puts one on each of our plates, then sits down. I can tell by the look in her eyes—she's waiting for me to speak.

"Celeste, there's something I've been meaning to tell you, ever since last night."

Her one eyebrow pops up. "Oh?"

"Well . . . you see, the thing is . . . oh hell, I'll just say it. I waited for you."

Her brow furrows. "Whaddya mean?"

I finally sit down to start eating. "I saved myself for you. I mean, you were my first."

She almost chokes on a bite of pancake before grabbing her orange juice to wash it down. "You mean, you were a virgin until last night?"

I nod slowly. "Yep."

"Wow, you could've fooled me."

"Well, let's just say, I've been studying up for the big day."

"I bet you have," she says, bouncing her eyebrows. "Wanna give mama some more of that sugar?"

Rising from her chair, she throws her clothes off, sashays around the table, slides onto my lap. She tongues the syrup from my lips, tittering, then frowns, gazing into my eyes.

That sudden turn from playful to serious kills me every time.

"How did I get so lucky?" I wonder.

"Well, you're about to get lucky, if that's what you mean." She glances down at my boxers, pulls at the waistband. "Take these off."

As soon as I do, she squirts syrup all over my chest, licking it off, sending a shiver through me. The spark of the idea is in her eyes as soon as I think of it. We rub syrup all over our skin, gluing ourselves together, laughing with abandon.

Then she gets serious again.

"Thank you."

"For what?"

"For giving me a sacred gift. I'll cherish it. Always." ←

my

†

Unfortunately, that cherished gift had long ago been discarded.

As I walked into Celeste's kitchen now, she pointed to a small round table in the corner, and I sat down. There were still remnants of egg dye and glitter on it.

I watched her at the sink. "Don't you guys have a dishwasher?"

Her head snapped around. "Ha! You're lookin' at her!"

"But I see one right next to you." Strange. I heard Elsie's tone in my voice.

"Oh, that thing? It's been broken for years. We can't afford a new one right now, and no matter how often I remind Mike to fix it, he never seems to get around to it."

I knew it. I knew I made more money than that son of a bitch. He's so full of shit. I bet I could've given Celeste a house at least twice the size of what they're living in now.

"That doesn't surprise me."

A ceramic bowl clinked at the bottom of the sink, and I wondered if she'd dropped it on purpose. "Look Dylie, I'm sorry about Mike. I had no idea he'd act like that."

"Yeah, what's his problem anyway?"

She stared out the window for a while, probably contemplating my question. I could hear Mike horsing around with the kids outside.

"I don't like the way he went about it either, but you have to understand how he feels. I mean, put yourself in his shoes for a moment. If the situation were reversed, you'd probably be bent out of shape too, if some ex-boyfriend came up for a visit, not knowing who he is or what his intentions are."

"I don't think so. I'd have you. I'd be fine."

She turned around. "You're missing the point, Dylie. He's very protective of his family—which I love about him—so in his mind, you're the interloper."

"Then why invite me up? We could've saved ourselves all this trouble if you'd never sent me that goddamn letter in the first place."

She rinsed the soap off her hands, and then dried them with a repurposed golf towel. Never taking her eyes off me, she stepped carefully toward the table, sat down, brushed some of the glitter onto the floor. Then, in a surprise move, she reached out for my left hand, stroking the top of it with her thumb, just like she used to do when we were together.

As if no time had passed at all.

Glancing off to the side, she got a faraway glaze in her eyes. "I have missed you, you know. If nothing else, I just wanted you to know that."

It took me a few moments to find my breath. Looking down at the table, I focused on a spot of green glitter, which reminded me of my dream from this morning. It gave me the courage to speak what had been in my heart for so long.

"Celeste, there isn't a day gone by I haven't thought of you, or wished you were still in my life. But you left me hangin', you know? I just can't get over the fact that you didn't want to be my wife. I mean, I thought we were perfect for each other, ya know?" I tried to choke down the sobs, but they charged out of my throat.

"Oh Dylie, I'm so sorry." She stood up and cradled my head to her stomach, her heart pulsing serenely there. The tears just kept coming, as if the dam of eight years had finally burst; as if the weight of all those memories were finally being released.

She stroked my hair while I held on to her for dear life. "Can you forgive me, even after all this time?"

I sniffled, bringing my head up slowly. Her compassion always astounded me. "I *can* forgive you, but it's myself I can't forgive. I mean, I fucked up big time. I let the love of my life slip away."

"Oh Dylie, you didn't do anything wrong. We just weren't meant to be."

"But why? It just doesn't make any sense."

She pressed my head into her sweatshirt, where I could smell the apples and cinnamon from the pies she'd made this morning. "Oh Dylie, don't you see? The reasons don't matter anymore. Only the love does."

I buried my face in her sweatshirt and kept bawling like a wounded child. She just stood there—stout as stone, yielding as water—while she hummed a low tune.

"And don't you think for a second that it was because of you. It wasn't you. You're an amazing person, and you deserve love. You deserve to be happy."

I wiped the tears from my cheeks, slowly pulling away from her. She sat down again, closer this time. "Is that why you invited me up here? Just to tell me that? That doesn't make any sense."

She let go of my hand, exhaling loudly, staring out the window again for a long time. The kids continued to scream and carry on outside.

"It's something that means we'll still be in each other's lives, just differently than either of us thought."

Lightning struck my gut. "For God's sake, Celeste, just tell me. Why all the secrecy?"

There was another long pause as she played with the sleeves of her sweatshirt, staring down at the table. "Okay, well, here goes." Her head seemed to move in slow motion, her eyes far behind. "Okay . . . so the thing is . . . Mike isn't Elsie's father."

That lightning traveled north, zapped my heart into a gallop. "Holy shit, Celeste. Are you saying what I think you're saying?"

She nodded slowly, her eyes filling up with tears.

"Does Mike know?"

She nodded again, almost imperceptibly.

"Oh my God, Celeste! What about Elsie?"

"We haven't told her, but I'm sure she senses it. That's why she's taken a shine to you so quickly. I think she knows."

"Jesus Christ, Celeste. This changes everything."

"I know. And that's why Mike's been so bent out of shape. He's afraid you're gonna take Elsie away from him." She sniffled, ran her sleeve under her nose. "I mean, can you blame him? He's all she's ever known as a father."

"And here I thought he was just afraid I was gonna take *you* away from him."

"Well, that's part of it too, but we talked before you came up. I told him he doesn't have to worry."

I was sure I felt my heart stop. "Seriously? Like, not at all?"

She gave me the most pitiful look. "We've been over this, Dylie. I mean, what we had was great, but that's over now. I just want us to be friends, you know? Isn't that enough?"

"No, hell no, not after what we went through. You know Celeste, no one's even come close to you."

When she took my hand again, I was amazed at the softness of her palms. "I'm sorry, Dylie, but I'm happy where I am. Despite what you may think, he's a great husband and father. I'd never leave him."

"But do you love him as much as you once loved me?"

Her eyes narrowed. "I don't think you want me to answer that, Dylie. It's only gonna hurt you more."

All I could do was rub her knuckles, trying vainly to hold on to our connection.

"But don't you see? We'll always be in each other's lives now, raising Elsie together."

That green glitter glinted into my eyes. I blinked rapidly, waiting for this unwanted dream to end.

"I think God has a different purpose in mind for us now. I've accepted that. Can you?"

I stared at her. I didn't know if I could. The light of our past connection was just too bright, too intense, more real than anything she could offer me now.

✝

The sun parachutes into the canyon of the Columbia River, the sky ablaze with rose and orange, golden rays shooting through purple clouds. The foothills of the Cascade Mountains deepen and bruise, while the river reflects the skyfire, funneling lava toward the Gorge Amphitheater.

Flames from the sunset burn in the nebulae of our eyes, while Celeste and I cuddle closer to keep warm, the evening's heat evaporating. The opening Spanish guitar of Sting's "Fragile" resonates throughout the canyon, delicate piano notes dancing in emerald and magenta on the concert stage. We rest on her blanket, shoulder blades to grass blades, our open hearts telegraphs to the stars and moon, as we stare at the canopy above us, the music rafting us away.

We submerge into fresh, clear waters, breathing through our open mouths, sinking deeper and deeper into the river, until we settle into the murky floor, flowering into lotus position. She wraps her legs around my ribs, locks her ankles at my tailbone. The energy of our orgasm fountains up our spines, explodes out of our crowns— releasing our spirits back into the womb of the cosmos.

The next morning, we're reborn into a radiant dawn.

Celeste appears part ghostly, part human, and it's eerily quiet, save for some bird chirps and fuzzy insect buzz.

She sits in one of the wooden chairs next to our cabin, staring out at the horizon, willing the sun to rise. I take another sip of my hazelnut coffee, enjoying its warm, creamy sweetness.

I want to imbibe this liquid sunrise forever.

"So . . . where are we headed next on Celeste's whirlwind adventure?"

She puts her index finger up to her closed lips. "Shhhh. Stay in the moment, Dylie. We can talk about that stuff later."

There's a pregnant moment of silence before she speaks again. I just wait, gazing at the gradually brightening sky.

"You know this moment is all there is, right?"

I chuckle. "Are you teaching a course in Zen philosophy today?"

"I'm serious, Dylie. I know how your mind works. You're constantly looking ahead to see what we're gonna do next, or after we do something, you're busy thinking about what happened, analyzing everything I did or said."

The coffee suddenly makes my stomach feel sour, bitterness rising to the back of my throat. I swallow hard to keep the bile down. "I'm sorry. I didn't realize that bothered you."

"Actually, it doesn't. But I'm worried about you. You spend all your time thinking about life instead of living it. Life isn't a laboratory, ya know."

"How insightful."

"Dylan, you don't have to get all defensive. I'm not attacking you."

In short, graceful movements, she places her mug on the ground, moves the table out of the way, then pushes her chair closer, resting her forearm on mine.

"Dylie, look at me."

I keep my head pointed down. Her gaze is too intense.

"LOOK AT ME!" She pulls my face toward her. Once I see those blue eyes, that big smile, I can't keep up my façade any longer.

And just like that, she has me again.

"Look, all I'm saying is, I love you, and I wanna see you happy."

"I *am* happy. I've never felt so damn good in all my life." I kiss her, her breath bittersweet, while I stroke her hair. "You know I'm happy because of you, right?"

"Well, as much as I'd like to take the credit, you're the one making yourself happy."

I wave off her comment. "Don't be modest, Celeste."

"Dylie, listen. You feel good because for the first time in your life, you've opened your heart to all of love's possibilities. I'm just the catalyst."

"So you're saying this is all just a chemical reaction? I'm a chemistry major, and even *I* don't believe that."

She rolls her eyes, leans her head back, and lets her mouth hang wide open, as if trying to catch flies.

"Don't be so literal, Dylan. You feel ecstatic cause you've let all your barriers come down. You've showed me your soul. I'm just reflecting it back to you."

"I guess I'll just have to take your word for it."

She pats my hand. "Good. Just stick it in that computer brain of yours and let me know what prints out."

I sip my coffee as I watch the sun ignite the clouds in hot pinks and reds. It slowly lifts over the Colorado River plateaus, highlighting shades of green and brown on their jagged slopes. The river illuminates the rocks, carrying the sun's rays to all the dark places in its path.

"I'm sorry, Celeste, but I don't ever want this time with you to end."

She nods solemnly, stands up, extends her hand toward me. "Come on, follow me."

I hesitate at first, but I can't resist her invitation. Taking her hand, I follow her down a grassy knoll toward a dirt trail, where we come to its edge and stop. She pivots to face me, her profile glowing orange, like a half moon close to the horizon.

"Don't think about the future right now. In this moment, you and I share eternity."

"But—"

"Shhh, no more talking. Let the silence speak for you."

I drink in the light overflowing, something cracking open inside. Celeste wipes away one of my tears, puts it in her mouth.

"You're in it now, I can tell."

I transmit all my love to Celeste, watching it swell and rise in the silence, as she receives it in her sunrise smile.

†

As the sun beamed down on me now, I sensed a new direction in the unfolding of events with Celeste. I had ignored it before, but now I felt it, pulsing faintly under the surface, as the inevitable current of our lives. Everything about our spiritual connection had an irrefutable course, its powerful flow leading me here, at last, to witness the beauty of her family. Perhaps our love was a blessing—not a curse—as I had assumed it was for so long.

Maybe this could work. I just had to give it a chance.

From the back patio deck, I watched Mike "hide" the plastic Easter eggs. He put most of them on the ground, on the tops of small bushes or in branch nooks of low-hanging trees, so I could tell he was stacking the deck in Luke's favor, but I didn't care. Elsie and I would still win.

He'd barely finished laying out the eggs before Luke and Elsie came sprinting onto the deck, shouting at each other, baskets in hand.

"Hey, wait! I wanna be fihst!" Luke exclaimed.

"Nah uh, ladies first!" Elsie tapped me on the arm. "Come on Dylie, we gotta start before Mikey's ready!"

It seemed strange that she called the man who was supposed to be her father by his first name, but she was already off and running before I could say anything. I leapt off the deck to chase after her.

"Dad, come ovah, quick! We-ah gonna wose if you don't huwy!"

I picked up a turquoise egg on the ground, then a bright orange one, and from behind a rock, a hot pink one. I shook all three like maracas, coins jangling in two of them, jellybeans clattering in the other. While she ~~bent over to pick~~ picked up a green egg, I placed my three in her basket. "Here ya go, Elsie," I said, "there's three more for ya!"

"Awesome! I know we're gonna win now!"

I spotted a yellow egg next to a bush and bent over to pick it up. But before I could stand again, something broke over my butt. At first, sharp shards poked through my jeans, then a gooey wetness ran down the back of my pants. That was when I knew—I'd just been hit. I figured Luke had done it, so I turned around to face the culprit.

"Ha ha, gotcha!" Mike yelled from the bottom of the porch stairs. Another egg whizzed by my head, followed by another one hitting the ground by my feet, exploding all over my sneakers. The eggs kept coming hard and fast, like in a batting cage, so I took off running. As he chased after me, the intensity of his eyes belied the playful expression on his face.

"Elsie, get as many eggs as you can! I'm under attack!"

Her face screwed up in concentration, she bolted to a seedling tree where several eggs had been attached with electrical tape. "That's not fair, Daddy! You can't do that!"

"All's fair in love and war, sweetie!" He threw another egg, but this one only glanced by my jacket. Luke got so caught up in the moment that he started throwing his own plastic eggs at me.

"No Luke, don't throw 'em! Keep yours and find the rest! You gotta beat your sister!" Mike bellowed, sounding like a football coach.

Elsie smiled at her brother's mistake, ~~scooping up~~ *grabbing* what he'd thrown on the ground. "Hey, no fay-ah! Give 'em back!" Luke cried.

He ran after her, but she was too fast for him. Even with the age difference, I couldn't believe how easily she'd outsmarted him.

"No Luke! She's tricked you! Disengage pursuit! Get the rest of the eggs!"

Panic flashed across his face, and he spun around to go the other way. Elsie kept giggling as she scooped up more eggs from the ground.

I wanted to throw something back at Mike, but I knew if I drew his attention away from Elsie, we'd win. His throws kept getting closer and closer, so I decided to bound up the deck steps, and as I jumped down the stairs to the other side, he whipped another egg. It splattered against the light blue aluminum siding, yolk dripping down the kitchen window.

"Mike, what the hell are you doing? You're gonna ruin the paint!" Celeste screamed from the kitchen.

"But it's Dylan's fault, honey! He's the one who moved his face out of the way!" Laughing uncontrollably, he chucked another egg at the window. It exploded, yolk and shell shards streaking down the glass, which had somehow remained unbroken.

"Michael!" she scolded. "You better not break any of the windows, or I'll march right out there and kick your ass!"

"Don't worry, honey, I'll clean it up," he said, still chuckling.

"You'd better! And I hope you didn't get Dylan's clothes dirty either!"

"He's fine, honey. That's what washin' machines are for!" He cocked his arm back to hurl another egg, but when he saw both kids running back with their baskets, he put his arm down. Even though the hunt was over, I could tell he wanted to smash one right over my head.

I strode up to him, goading him to do it. He had the height and weight advantage, but I didn't care; I'd been itching for a fight ever since I got here. I couldn't wait to splatter egg all over his stupid face.

His eyes narrowed. "Go ahead, Dylan. Show everybody the man you really are."

I was about to lunge toward him, but Elsie grabbed my arm, pulling me down to her level.

Her blue eyes entreated me. "Dylie, no. We won," she whispered. "Be the better man."

I still wanted to punch him, but she was right—perhaps she *was* smarter than the rest of us. Besides, I wanted to keep making a good impression on my daughter.

As I backed away and stood up, Elsie exclaimed, "We won, we won!"

"Nah uh, I did!" Luke shouted back.

"You can't even count 'em right, dummy."

"Yes I can. You ah wi-ah!"

"All right kids, that's enough," Mike intervened. "Let's count 'em up to see who got the most." He looked back at the kitchen. "Hey Hon! How many eggs did we put out here?"

"Fifty."

"Okay . . . so Elsie, how many do you—"

"Thirty-three!"

"Wow, that's very good. And how many did you get, Luke?"

He was busy adding them up. At one point he lost count, so he had to start over. He scratched his head and tried to concentrate.

"See, I told you he couldn't count."

"Shut up! Can to!"

"You have seventeen there," she said, pointing into his basket. "There's no need to count them."

Luke's face lit up in amazement, like his sister had just performed a magic trick. "How'd you know?"

"Fifty minus thirty-three equals seventeen. DUH!"

"I hate you!" Luke dropped his basket, some of the eggs rolling out the side. He charged at her, but when I stepped between them, he stopped in his tracks.

"Calm down, Luke," I said, suddenly aware of my towering height. "There's no need to get upset. We'll share some of our candy with you. Isn't that right, Elsie?"

"Says who? I'll share some with *you*, Dylie, but I'm definitely *not* sharing with that little toad."

Before Luke could go after her again, Mike came from behind, gripping his shoulders like a vise. For a moment, I thought he'd try to restrain me too. "Elsie, stop trying to *egg* on your little brother."

Elsie and I rolled our eyes.

109

"Michael, get your butt in here!" Celeste called out from the screen door.

"Oooooooooh. Daddy's in trouble, Daddy's in trouble," Elsie sing-songed.

He put his hands up to his head like antlers, waved his fingers at her, stuck out his tongue. Elsie mimicked the gesture, and they both laughed. Keeping his tongue out, he scowled at me, then sauntered up the stairs, slithered into the house.

"I can't believe you're acting like this!" *also yells*

Luke looked scared, but Elsie just rolled her eyes. "See, the thing you gotta know about Mommy is, she gets mad at everybody."

I chuckled. "I see what you mean!"

For the first time, I pondered the reality of being married to Celeste. Would she be yelling at me as often as stupid Mike?

Elsie grabbed my hand. "Come on, Daddy, let's go in!"

I gazed at her, my mouth hanging wide open. "What did you say?"

She smiled knowingly, winking at me. "You heard me. Don't act like you don't know."

I studied her face for any traces of a joke, but there were none. If I hadn't believed it when Celeste told me, I believed it now.

"Come on, Daddy. Let's get what's rightfully ours."

†

"Jeez, I hope you never turn out like that when *you* become a dad," Celeste says on our drive to her Junior Prom.

Senior ?

110

My laughter halts. "You think I'll be a dad someday?"

"Definitely. You'll make a great father for our daughter."

Her face performs that sudden pivot from frivolous to serious that I love so much. Most guys at sixteen would be petrified at the thought of being a dad, but not me. Not with Celeste. I already know she's the One.

"Aren't we a bit presumptuous?"

She giggles. "Maybe."

"And how do you know it'll be a girl? What if it's a boy?"

"I'd be okay with that too, as long as we're together, raising our child."

"And did you dream this too?"

"Maybe."

She puts her hand on my left thigh, handling it like a fragile object. While we wait at a red light, she looks at me, smiles with just her lips, and widens her eyes to take me all in, like light into a camera lens.

To this day, I've never felt so loved.

Back in the dining room, †

As I stared at Celeste, I wondered where all that love had gone. I prayed there was still some left for me.

"Okay kids," Celeste began in her autocratic voice. "You should each take five pieces of candy at a time and put them in your baskets. That way, you both get an equal amount of candy."

"Come on, Mom, this isn't China," Elsie said.

"Ooh hon, she's calling you a communist country— pretty harsh!" Mike snickered.

Celeste hit him. "Stop it. Not everything's a joke."

"And life isn't always fair," Elsie whined. "I should get all the stuff I won. This sucks."

"I wouldn't do that if I were you, Elsie," Mike warned. "Look! Your brother's already grabbin' everything he can!"

"That's because he can't count . . . hey, wait! Let me get some!" While Luke picked out one or two pieces of candy at a time, she swept candy into her basket with her longer arms.

"Elsie, stop that!" Celeste said. "Do it one at a time like your brother!"

"Oh, come on! Why do you favor him so much?"

"Keep backtalking me, young lady. Meanwhile, your brother's stealing all your candy."

"Crap! No fair!"

I laughed as Elsie went after my favorite candy—the Reese's Peanut Butter Cups—as greedily as I had when I was a kid. Perhaps we were more alike than I'd realized.

"There, that should keep 'em busy for a while," Celeste said, turning her glare to Mike. "And as for you, mister, you need to clean up your big mess."

He flashed his best poker face. "It can wait."

Her eyebrows rose. "Well, you could, but it'll be a lot easier to clean up while it's wet. If you wait till it dries, you'll have to get the scraper out."

I knew I shouldn't be laughing right now, but I couldn't help it. As far as I was concerned, Mike was finally getting his comeuppance.

His face burning red, he grabbed a bucket and rag from under the kitchen sink and stormed out, the screen door closing behind him like a thrown fist. Fortunately, the kids didn't even notice; they were too absorbed in hoarding candy.

"You certainly told him," I said, chuckling.

"Well if I don't, who will?"

She stared outside for a moment, lost in thought.

"Actually, I'd better go check on him. If I don't supervise, he won't do a good job."

"Seriously?"

"It's all too true, I'm sorry to say." She paused, still looking outside. "Hey, do you mind watching the kids while I'm supervising Mike? They shouldn't be too much trouble. You'll just have to make sure they don't eat too much candy."

"Sure, no problem."

Her smile disappeared as she marched out the patio door.

While she got serious, I was amused. I couldn't tell if Mike was just a slacker, or if Celeste had him henpecked. Either way, I was glad I wasn't being forced to do something I didn't want to do. Then again, I wouldn't have thrown eggs at the house in the first place.

Elsie and Luke had already started eating their candy. I thought of reprimanding them, but then I got an idea. If I wanted to prove to Celeste that I could be good with her kids, and again show her I was better than Mike, this was my chance.

"Hey guys, why don't we play a card game, see who can win the most goodies?"

The kids turned toward me, brown all over their mouths and hands. They looked like chocolate clowns.

"That's actually a good idea," Elsie said. "I like the way you think. Now I'll definitely win." She looked right through me. "*Daddy.*"

Luke stared at her. "What ah you tawking about? Daddy's outside."

As if on cue, Mike bellowed, "Jesus Christ, Celeste, why are you acting like this? You're being fucking ridiculous!"

Elsie glared at Luke. "I said 'Dylie.' Do you need to get your ears checked? So, what'd you have in mind, *Dylie*?"

"You guys ever play 21?"

"No," Elsie replied, "but I saw Bugs Bunny play it a few times on TV."

"I nev-ah heawd of it."

"Don't worry Luke, it's easy to play." I sat down at the dining room table, swept all the uneaten candy to the center. "Okay guys, we're gonna put all the goodies in the middle, and divide them up evenly among the three of us."

"Hey wait, that's not fair. You're just like Mommy!"

If only.

"Actually Elsie, it is fair. We're gonna use our money and candy as betting chips, so by the end of the game, it's possible to have more candy than anyone else."

She thought about this idea for a while, then her eyes lit up. "Ooh, I like that game."

"I knew you would."

She pulled out the playing cards—seemingly out of nowhere—like another magic trick. I wondered if she had sensed my plan, long before I even said anything. Trying to shake off her apparent clairvoyance, I brushed a pile of candy over to each of them. They kept eyeing up each other's stash.

It took a few minutes to explain the rules of the game, but as soon as I said, "Hit me!" Luke punched Elsie's arm. "Ow, you little brat, that hurt."

As he was laughing, she raised her fist to hit him back.

"Now Elsie, don't retaliate. Remember what you told me outside."

She held her fist in the air while Luke cowered down, then slowly lowered her arm, a smirk tracing across her face. "Okay, Dylie. We'll play it your way."

"That's my girl! All right, so let's put one piece of candy out in the center to bet. That's called an ante."

"But I haven't even looked at my cards yet."

"Don't worry, Elsie, you can make another bet once you look at 'em. For now, we each have to pay our way into the round." I put a Hershey's Kiss in the pot.

She followed with a purple Jolly Rancher. "I'm giving you the candy I don't like. I think the grape ones are gross."

Luke was going to put a Reese's Miniature in, but after hearing what his sister said, he put in a black jellybean instead. "Yeah, the bwack ones ah gwoss."

I chuckled. "Okay Luke, you'll have to put two of those in. Two jellybeans equal one Jolly Rancher." I held up both candies for a size comparison.

"Oh, okay. I see now."

While he put another black jellybean in, Elsie looked down—with a disapproving glance—at my one lone Kiss in the pot. I knew I'd better throw another one in before she called me out. Like Celeste, she was a stickler for the rules.

"Great, now we're all ready to play!" I shuffled the deck, dealt the cards. Both of them took their cards and slid them toward the edge of the table, peering their heads down to peek at what they had. Luke's face lit up, telegraphing his hand, but Elsie already had an impressive poker face.

"You know, even though this is your game, I'm still gonna beat you."

"Oh really? *yeah, Elsie?* Well then, put your candy where your mouth is!"

I put three Jolly Ranchers in the pot. Luke counted on his fingers, then put in six black and white jellybeans. Elsie shoved in six grape Jolly Ranchers, revealing her cards before I could stop her. She had an Ace of Diamonds and a Queen of Hearts. Leaning back in her chair, she crossed her arms smugly.

Oh man, were Luke and I in for it. She raked in her candy, then threw a purple Jolly Rancher at Luke's chest, where it bounced off and clattered on the floor. I thought he would get mad, but instead, he giggled, hurling black jellybeans at Elsie. She ducked as they whizzed by her head into the kitchen. It wasn't long before it was an all-out candy war.

I joined in, unable to help myself.

Celeste yelled from outside, "You agreed to do this, Mike! You can't back out now!"

I laughed, wondering if Celeste and Mike were arguing because of me.

Part of me hoped I was right.

†

After an interminable wait, the magical moment finally arrives. For what feels like forever, I've been staring at the back of Celeste's green sweater, fidgeting in the seat behind her.

As I open her valentine, I'm a little disappointed that she only gave me one, but at least it's bigger than the cards from the other girls. And little do I know, she's harboring a secret surprise.

Finally, she turns to face me, flashing her radiant smile. Giggling, she splays out my valentines like a deck of cards. "Three! Wow, you must really like me."

"I wanted to give you a thousand, but I didn't think they'd all fit."

"I bet. Go ahead. Open mine!"

I tear open the envelope. Shaped like a pink candy heart, the front of the card says, "Hug me!"

My heart skips a couple beats. "What, you mean now?"

She chuckles. "No, silly. That's for later. Read what's inside."

Flipping it open, I see one burning question written in thick purple marker: "Will you go to Prom with me?"

I read it several times to make sure I'm not hallucinating. My throat dries out, and I have to swallow several times before I can speak. "Seriously? We're only like, in second grade."

She laughs like that's the silliest thing she's ever heard. "So? Why not get my date early?"

As if she's already dreamed this moment into existence, Celeste stands up, steps intently toward me. I embrace her, breathing in her coconut-scented hair and the cherry Lifesaver she's sucking on. I never want to let her go. As

The words just pop out (;) ~~before I can stop them~~: "I love you."

Like a bomb has just exploded, my confession blasts me away from her. But then—mysteriously, magically—she grabs me by the shoulders, pulls me to her again, and presses our lips together. We stare at each other, wide-eyed, not daring to blink. My ~~ribs~~ feel like ~~they're melting into~~ chocolate, melting heart from the heat of her kiss.

117

Before I can even process what's happened, and before I can even think about stopping her, she sprints out into the hallway.

Paralyzed by her kiss, I just stand there, gaping, my face as red as Celeste's valentine.

Even now, I wish I had followed her. And actually taken her to Senior Prom. Then maybe—just maybe—this whole other reality might not have played out.

†

When Celeste and Mike finally burst in—red-faced and winded—I wondered if they'd been fighting that whole time, or sneaked in a round of make-up sex in the backyard. Had it been any other couple, I would've applauded their sense of carpe diem, but this was Celeste, who, despite our healing moment in the kitchen, was still the one that had gotten away.

Back at the table, Elsie was winning by a mile. She had a small mountain of candy on her side, and Luke had only a molehill, which was quickly dwindling. I had next to nothing, purposely hitting on any number except 21, just so I'd bust and they'd win. But even during the times when I actually gave it my best effort, Elsie still beat me most of the time. She seemed to have a knack for games, no matter what we played. She must've gotten that competitive edge from Celeste, who had decisively beaten me at the Love Game of Love.

"I noticed some of your Easter candy on the floor back there," Celeste said, scowling. "So. Who started it?"

"It was Dylie's idea, Mommy."

Celeste glared at me. "Is this true, Dylan?"

I couldn't believe my little girl had sold me out. "Well, I didn't start it, but I sure did finish it!"

When everyone laughed except Celeste, I realized that maybe Mike was right. Maybe she *was* too serious for her own good.

She put her hands on her hips, tapping her right foot. "I see. I guess Mike's not the only big kid around here."

I could tell Mike was still in the doghouse. He handed her a glass of water, apparently unwilling to even make eye contact. This was a side of Celeste I'd never seen. I knew Mike was an idiot, and probably deserved a scolding, but I couldn't help wondering if I were her husband, would I be playing the same pathetic role as him? I hoped not.

Yet I was starting to think that fate had saved me from a potentially bad relationship. Perhaps Celeste was right too. Perhaps everything had worked out, just like it was supposed to. I just had to trust there was a better plan for me.

"So, what trouble have you gotten my kids into?" Celeste demanded.

"We're playing Blackjack for candy."

"You know it'll never be fair that way. Elsie'll win almost every time."

"Well, that's fine. I'll give the rest of my candy to Luke. I wouldn't want to start another war."

"God knows we have enough of those," she said, staring at Mike, who still wasn't making eye contact. "Mind if I join you guys? This looks fun."

I stood up, waved to my open seat. "By all means, Celeste, but I think I'm gonna take a break. Elsie's really cleaning my clock."

"See, I *told* you I'd beat you at your own game."

"Yeah yeah, I know."

Mike pointed toward the living room. "Hey Dylan, wanna catch the hockey game on TV?"

Celeste's eyes widened. "Be careful," she mouthed.

I nodded, following him out of the kitchen. Whatever he had to say, I knew I wasn't going to like it. ~~one bit~~

†

"What about Mike?" I ask Celeste, as we drive back to the sacred spot of our first kiss. "Do I have to worry about him?"

"No. Of course not."

"But how do I know you guys won't get back together?"

"Trust me. You don't have to worry about *that*."

"I do trust you, Celeste. It's him I don't."

"Look. Obviously, if he had his way, we'd still be together. But I don't want that. When we broke up, I told him we have different priorities in life."

"Meaning what, exactly?"

She squeezes my hand. "Meaning . . . you shouldn't worry so damn much. That's your problem, Dylie. You overthink everything."

Steering into Manito Park, she parks the car and kills the engine. But as always, she leaves the stereo on, knowing it might be broadcasting an important message, just for us. Right on cue, Frou Frou's "Let Go" charges the silence between us, reminding me of *Garden State*, one of our favorite movies to watch together.

"Lean your seat back," she instructs.

I push it back as she sits on my lap. Then she kisses me in that slow, simmering way I can't get enough of.

"I want you to promise me something," she says solemnly, her eyes wild in the dark.

"Sure. Anything."

"Promise me you'll just let go. Promise me you'll just jump into this moment. And never look back."

There she is again, perfectly tuned into the song, infusing this moment with meaning. That uncanny connection to music would always connect me to her, no matter the physical or emotional distance between us.

"Okay. That's not hard."

She raises both eyebrows. "Come on, Dylie. I know you. You're so serious all the time. You need to lighten up."

I nod and look down at the floor, trying not to act offended. "Okay. Deal."

"Awesome, let's go!" she squeals, throwing open the passenger door and slipping out into the night.

What could I do but follow her?

†

I followed Mike into the living room, the sun streaming through the bay window. He popped off his shoes, his size fourteens thudding on the floor, then reclined his chair and flipped on the hockey game. The roar of the crowd filled the small space of the room, and as he started rooting for the Carolina Hurricanes, I silently picked the New Jersey Devils. For several minutes we didn't talk, our eyes trained on the TV. The Hurricanes were posting a 3-0 shutout, and I desperately needed a comeback victory right now.

Because I knew Mike and I were locked in our own high-stakes competition—he had Celeste, and I had Elsie. In the end, I wondered who would score the winning goal.

He set the remote down on the arm of his chair. "Look, Dylan, there's a reason I wanted it to be just you and me in here."

Here we go. "Oh?" I said, sitting down on the couch next to his chair.

"Yeah, I can tell you're havin' a hard time with everything. But I just wanted you to know, you shouldn't feel bad. Believe me, there are times when *I'm* jealous of *you*."

"What? I don't believe that for a second."

"Seriously, dude. I may've gotten Celeste, but you got your freedom. You got to do whatever the hell you wanted for the last eight years, while I had to grow up fast and be a dad. Don't get me wrong, I wouldn't trade it for anything, but there are some days I wish I could be in your shoes. Like today, know what I mean?"

He winked at me, but I just shook my head. "Actually, my life hasn't been all that exciting. I went to grad school, traveled a bit, played small band and DJ gigs. But I ain't no rock star."

"You don't have to be, man, that's the thing. You got your freedom. You should be grateful."

"I just wish things would've turned out differently, ya know?"

"Well then, you woulda been a daddy all this time. You honestly think you're ready for that?"

"I've been ready for the last eight years."

"Uh huh." He stared at me intensely. "Look dude, I know. I know she's yours."

"I don't know what you're talking about."

"Come off it, Dylan. You're tellin' me you woulda buckled down and been a daddy if Celeste had told you?"

"In a heartbeat."

"I don't think so. A free spirit like you, you woulda gotten antsy and resentful. It woulda been a burden."

"You don't know me."

"Maybe not, but I've known guys like you, guys who felt pinned and trapped after a *few weeks* of fatherhood." He placed the remote on his belly, watched it rise and fall. "All I'm sayin' is, Celeste gave you a gift. I just hope someday you have the sense to accept it, ya know?"

My stomach burned. "Did Celeste put you up to this?"

"Yeah right. She ain't the boss of me."

I smirked. "I think that egg incident proves otherwise."

He eyed me like a Wild-West gunslinger, then exhaled heavily, mumbling something under his breath. All I heard was "goddammit."

"What was that?"

"Nothin', man. Look . . . all I'm sayin' is, she's givin' you another gift now, if you'd just open your fuckin' eyes to see it! You're too busy lookin' for something that has to come in just the right package."

"Ok Mike, if you say so."

"Look, she invited you up here to share in Elsie's life. You know that, right?"

"Of course. That's obvious now."

"Good. All I'm sayin' is, she's opened the door for ya. Are ya gonna walk through it?"

"Will you let me?"

He glared at me the same way Celeste had, right after he made his big egg mess. "I'm not gonna stand in your way when it comes to Elsie. If the situation was reversed, I hope you'd do the same for me."

I acted like I was watching the game. "I don't know if I could."

"And see, that's the difference between you and me. I'm holdin' the door *wide* open for ya."

"Wow Mike, you're so magnanimous."

"Look, I'll level with you. I wanted you to come up to see if I could trust you. That's why I left you alone with Celeste and Elsie, why I gave you shit at dinner, why I threw eggs at you. I wanted to test you, ya know, see if you're as good a man as Celeste says you are."

My heart soared knowing that Celeste still saw me as a good person. "Well teach, did I pass?"

The Devils just scored their second goal, and I inwardly rejoiced. Maybe they would actually come back to win, or at least tie. Anything would be better than another loss to Mike.

"Look man, I know what you two *had* was special. But the reality is, she's with me now, and that's the way it's gotta be. I mean, don't you have a girl back home?"

"Of course," I lied. "But she's not Celeste."

"Well then, the sooner you accept that Celeste will never be yours again, the better off we'll *all* be."

"I'll keep that in mind."

"Dylan, listen. You have a choice. You can either continue to think of her as your girlfriend, make yourself miserable in the process, and push her farther away, or you can accept the friendship she's offerin' you. And with Elsie as part of the deal, you'd be a *fool* not to take it."

"I don't need your advice. I can deal with this myself."

He rolled his eyes, snorted. "Look dude, all I'm sayin' is, there's a whole world of chicks out there, and you're here pinin' for the one you can't have. Just doesn't make any sense, ya know?"

"Yeah, well, love doesn't much make sense, ya know?"

"Makes perfect sense to me. You open yourself to givin' and receivin' love. What else is there?"

"It's not that simple."

"Of course it is. You're the one making it complicated."

I finally volleyed back his gaze. "It's not me. It's the situation. If you weren't here, everything would be hell of a lot simpler."

He shook his head. "But that's not the way things *are*, man. That's your problem, Dylan. You can't accept reality."

"That's because reality sucks."

"Maybe for you. But it could be better—a lot better—if you'd just be grateful for what God's given you."

I sat straight up, threw my hands into the air. "And what great things has God given me, huh? I can't *wait* to hear this."

His head sagged as he sighed. "Now I see why Celeste dumped you. You're just impossible to please."

"That's it. I don't have to take this from you." I stood up. "I'm outta here."

Mike's voice lowered. "You walk outta here, that's it. There ain't no comin' back."

"What the hell are you talking about?"

His eyes blazed, his jaw tightened. "I'm serious. You leave, that's it. You don't get invited back."

"I don't need your charity."

I turned toward the door, but before I could even take a step, he grabbed my right arm. His grip seemed superhuman. I tried to wrestle free, but couldn't.

"Open your fuckin' eyes, Dylan! God's givin' you a new life with Celeste and Elsie, if you'd just get over your stubborn self already! Don't you see? He's givin' you the green light, man. So stop runnin' yourself through the red light into a ditch."

Mike finally released my arm, but then some force much stronger than muscle tension was holding me in place—it was the paradox of a dream grounding me firmly in reality. Whether he knew it or not, he'd tapped into both my dream from this morning and Bolt's Edenic vision from Good Friday.

So I just stood there—lost in reverie—watching the sun set through the bay window, as dust particles floated in a river of golden light.

†

Garnet specks in the oval-shaped rocks sparkle in the dying sunlight, dancing to a silent symphony broadcast from another dimension. While the rocks infuse the sand in rose shades, a fog rolls in, wrapping the sea stacks in shrouds of mystery.

Once again, Celeste has taken me to a sacred place. A place where only love can flourish.

We sit on a large piece of white driftwood—one of many in this wooden graveyard—watching the moon siphon light from the sun. I look out into the dark ocean, then to Celeste, whose eyes reflect the blooming stars. My words seem to come from another place.

"In the horizon of our love, I see infinite possibilities."

She stares at me for a moment, her face blank at first, then a smile slowly stretches over her cheeks. "Oh my little poet, you always know the right thing to say."

When she kisses me, her lips feel like soft paintbrushes. "And to think, you claim to be a scientist. I don't buy it for a second."

My laughter spills out. "Well, I have been thinking about becoming a musician lately, thanks to your influence."

"You should, or at least a DJ or something. You definitely have a strong connection to music."

Celeste's words propel me into the future—I'm a DJ in front of a large crowd, playing the most electrifying music. Diamonds flash in my mind, then blind me. Everything washes out in white.

She shakes my arm. "Hey Dylie, you still with me?"

"Yeah, sorry, I just feel so connected to everything right now. It must be the full moon, the beach and you, all conspiring to seduce me."

"You know Dylie, you can feel all that without the moon, or me. It's just like I told you back in Paradise. It's all right in here."

Her finger drills into my sternum; I squirm.

"You don't need anyone or anything else to feel it. You just decide you wanna be happy, and you can be. It's that simple."

I shake my head slowly from side to side. "If it were that easy, I'd be happy all the time."

"Well, someday you'll realize you have all the love you need. I'm just here to draw it out of you."

"Wait . . . what're you saying? Is this a breakup talk?"

She grabs my hands, strokes them softly. Her eyes look ready to burst. "I just don't want you to depend on me to feel good. With or without me, you're a good person, and you deserve to be happy."

I nod solemnly, peering at the largest sea stack, a nebula of fog enshrouding it. The moon beams down between bands of fish-scale clouds, and I close my eyes, breathing in salt and sulfur, crashing waves rolling through my ears.

When I reopen my eyes, she's staring at me expectantly, compelling me to speak. "You're just the center of my universe right now. Why would I want that to change?"

Her finger points at my chest again. "*You* should be the center of *your* universe. I'm just in orbit for now."

"Well, don't leave. I got plenty of sunlight for you yet."

"Come on, let's go out to the water. I dreamed about this, and I wanna make it a reality."

"Wait . . . I thought we weren't allowed to go swimming."

She cocks her right eyebrow, a smirk sneaking up the same side. "Oh my dear Dylan, do you always do what you're told?"

"Well, it *is* usually safer that way."

As evidence for my caution, I point to the couples walking on the beach. "But what about those people? What if they see us?"

Her other eyebrow rises. "Do you really think they'll care? They're probably gonna jump in later anyway."

"I dunno. You sure it's safe?"

"Come on Dylie, it's our last night on the road. Don't you wanna make it special?"

"Of course."

"Well then, let's go. It'll be another first! I'll totally make it worth your while."

Her spontaneous spirit is contagious. I take her hand as we head toward the water. We tread barefoot over stones, then run when we hit the sand, ducking behind one of the stone pillars. She begins to disrobe.

"Wait . . . are you crazy?"

She laughs. "No, just horny."

"But aren't there riptides out there? And it looks awful cold too."

"Do you wanna get laid or not?"

I quickly throw my clothes into the breeze, but when I see her naked, I freeze. I just stand there—transfixed—watching her beautiful body gleam in the moonlight.

"Come on. Let's make this idea a reality."

We race arm-in-arm into the ocean, but as soon as our feet touch the water, we immediately change our minds. The cold almost steals my breath, sending chills through me.

"Holy shit that's cold!" I yell, yanking her out like she's attached to a bungee cord.

"Oh my God, I had no idea!" she cries, gripping my hand tightly.

We sprint back to our stone pillar, and as soon as we get there, I instinctively reach for my clothes.

"Wait," she implores, grabbing my arm. "Let's do it here."

"What? Seriously? What if someone sees us?"

"So what? It's getting dark, and no one will see us anyway. Besides, remember what I said about living in the moment?"

Needing no further encouragement, I pick her up, press her into the rock, and wrap her legs around my waist. I have never seen her smile so big.

"That's the spirit, Dylie!" She kisses me hard, then stares at me intensely. "But enough foreplay. I want you."

She reaches down, guides me inside. Her warmth is the greatest thrill I've ever known.

We join together in eternal, ecstatic prayer—rejoicing—for now we breathe as one organism, one spirit.

As Live's "The Dolphin's Cry" surges into my head, I raise her up—ever higher—as a sacred offering to the gods.

I have never felt so free.

†

But now I felt caged, trapped, ready to jump out of my skin. In this house, with this family, there was nowhere I could go, nowhere I could escape, without the past surging back to life.

"I think I'm gonna go now," I say regretfully.

Mike didn't turn from the TV. "Don't ya wanna see who wins?"

I didn't, because he'd already won. What else did I need to see?

Besides, the Hurricanes were still up 3-2, and they had control of the puck with only seconds left. So much for my comeback victory.

"Nah. The game's pretty much over anyway."

"You know you can stay here tonight too," he said, grimacing. "I mean, really, it's no problem."

"Thanks, but I already made reservations for a place in town. Besides, I wanna do some exploring on my own, check out this meditation center I saw online."

He went back to the game. "Okay, well, do what you want to."

I was already walking toward the door.

"Honey, kids, Dylan's leaving!"

I heard chairs squealing on the kitchen floor, then the patter of little feet.

"Wait, don't go!" Elsie cried. She came sprinting down the hallway, her flip-flops clacking on the floor. As soon as she saw me leaving, she hooked onto my legs, her bright blue eyes watering. I almost changed my mind right there on the spot.

"Don't worry, I'll be back. I just have to go into town and check in at the hostel."

"Hostel?" she replied, still gazing up at me. "They're dirty. You should stay here." She glared at Mike. "Did you do this?"

He laughed, his eyes still glued to the TV. "Don't look at me, sweetie. I told him he could stay."

"So stay. We all want you to."

It took all my will power not to give in. "Don't worry, sweetie, I'll be back tomorrow."

Like a master illusionist, she handed me a green plastic egg out of nowhere. "Well, if you just *have* to leave, then take this. It'll keep you safe."

"Oh really? Is it a magic egg?"

"Of course it is, silly. What else would it be?" She sprinted back into the kitchen.

I already missed her warmth.

When I shook Mike's hand, he still gave me that iron grip. Smacking me hard on the back, he leaned in and whispered, "I hope you seriously consider what we talked about."

Celeste didn't seem to hear his comment. She stepped into the room, embraced me. "You are coming back though, right? We all want to see you before you leave town."

"Yeah, I'll definitely be back tomorrow."

"Well, where will you stay?"

"I already got a hostel lined up."

"A hostel?" Celeste's voice sounded suspiciously like her daughter's. "We can spot you some money if you want to stay somewhere nicer."

Mike shot me a sideways glance, smirking. I shook my head. I guess he didn't understand the value of saving money.

"No really, I'm fine."

"Well, do you need any recommendations?" Celeste continued. "We know some good places to eat."

"Thanks, but I just like to wander around a bit, you know, find my way."

"See, I *told* you you were a free spirit," Mike said. I just rolled my eyes.

Elsie came running back from the kitchen, shoving some Reese's Miniatures into my hands. "Here, take some for the road."

"Why thank you, sweetie." I pocketed the candy, picked her up, and twirled her around until her neon green flip-flops almost flew off. Then I kissed her cheek, set her down carefully.

"Don't be a stranger," she said, wagging her index finger.

"Okay, I won't," I replied, trying to laugh instead of cry.

Before I could even open the screen door, I felt a tug on my shirt.

"I miss you already, Daddy," she said, rubbing her eyes.

My throat stung. "I'm gonna miss you too, sweetie."

"Be careful, Dylie," Celeste said. "Let us know if you need anything."

I nodded, gazing into Celeste's eyes, for what seemed like the last time. The whoosh of the screen door surprised me. I was already outside.

I trudged out to my car. The snow picked up, falling in fat flakes, the sky growing dark. Some impulse made me look back at the bay window. Elsie had her hands curved around the corners of her eyes, like peering through binoculars, while Celeste stood over top of her, waving and smiling. Elsie blew me a kiss. As I returned her gesture, I indulged in a moment of fantasy—I was just heading off to work, my wife and daughter saying goodbye, anxious for me to come back home.

†

Clearly, this place wasn't home. I realized that now.

Celeste and Elsie's faces were rapidly dissolving in an alcohol brain bath, while a man dressed in black jeans, a Van Halen T-shirt, and a leather jacket slowly approached me. He had a beer gut, thick glasses, and stubbly, chubby cheeks.

"Hey man, mind if I sit here?"

"Sure, have a seat. I'm Dylan."

He sat down, shook my hand. "Call me Eddie. Like Van Halen."

"Really? That's your name?"

"No, it's Van Heusen, but it's pretty close, and the name's cooler anyway."

"Okay, sure."

He set down his overflowing mug, chuckling at my four empty beer bottles. "Someone's gettin' an early start to the night."

"Yeah, well, it's been quite a day. I just visited my ex and found out I have a daughter."

He swigged his beer. "Shit, dude. You mean like, you didn't know?"

"Nope. And it's been eight years."

His black, bushy eyebrows rose. "Jesus. She waited that long to tell you?"

"Yeah, basically. And the worst part is, she's married to someone else."

"Bummer, dude."

"Yeah, tell me about it."

"Well, at least you got your freedom, right? Do you have to pay child support?"

I paused for a moment. I hadn't even considered child support until now, but I didn't mind the idea. Not at all. I'd do anything for Elsie and Celeste. And anything to show up Mike.

"Not yet."

"Well, consider yourself lucky then. Believe me, there are plenty more chicks out there, especially ones without a kid in tow."

I chuckled. It was beginning to sound like a conspiracy, as if Mike had organized a town hall meeting with all the single dudes, just so they could give me the same trite advice. I didn't want to argue and ruin my buzz, though.

"Yeah, I guess you're right."

He nodded vigorously. "In the meantime, you want some more liquid therapy?"

I peered into the neck of my beer bottle. "Yeah man, sounds good. I'm drinkin' Molsen."

"All right, I'll get it for ya."

I handed him a Canadian ten. "Here ya go."

He waved my hand away. "No need. My friend owns the bar. I get free drinks."

"Hey, that's cool. At least something's going right today."

He lumbered up to the bar, slammed his glass on the counter. A young, skinny bartender with a purple Mohawk, a bull nose ring, and nail-like earrings nodded at him. In less than a minute, Eddie brought back both beers. "Here ya go."

"Thanks, man."

The DJ's voice boomed over the PA system: "Good evening ladies and gentlemen. This is DJ Dan, and welcome to karaoke night here at Finley's. I see we have our typical Sunday crowd, so you have less people to embarrass yourself in front of."

It was a tired line; nobody laughed. He scanned the crowd for potential singers.

"Anyways, let's get started, eh? Our first and only singer so far is Dylan, singing Bob Dylan." He gave me a sideways glance, rolled his eyes. "How appropriate. He'll be singing 'Rainy Day Women.'"

I looked over at Eddie. "Wanna sing it with me so I don't look like too much of an idiot up there?"

"Oh man, I don't know. I'm not nearly drunk enough yet."

"Come on man, I share the guy's name for Christ's sake."

"Oh, all right." He chugged the rest of his beer, slapped it hard on the table, wiped his mouth with the back of his sleeve. "Okay, I'm ready."

We staggered up to the stage, grabbed our microphones, and tried out our best Bob Dylan impressions. Belting out the lyrics, we were even more off-key than Dylan was, but we didn't care. And judging by the non-reaction from our sparse audience, they didn't care either.

That was fine with me. Because for once, I was actually starting to forget about Celeste.

But when we got to the chorus, I wished I *were* stoned. I remembered this was the song I'd performed for her during our Pittsburgh weekend thirteen years ago.

I remembered how we dressed up and held our own private prom; how she laughed at my karaoke antics; how we slow-danced afterward, kissing softly. She'd even cried in my arms, grieving for her lost mother. In a strange reversal, I was now the one being consoled. She whispered in my ears, *The past is dead, the past is dead. You can't resurrect it.*

Whether I wanted to admit it or not, she was right. Hell, even Mike was right. I had to let go of her. I had to stop chasing ghosts. In pursuing her for the last twenty years, I'd become a ghost myself.

I realized now. I was dead inside.

But now it was time to wake up. Now it was time to chase after something else, something shimmering, something pulsating—just under the surface of things. I didn't know what it was, but its presence was unmistakable.

When the music switched over to "Walk Like an Egyptian," I smiled knowingly. Handing the mike back to the DJ, I waved goodbye to Eddie, flew out the door into the cold. I didn't know where I was headed, or what I was doing, but I knew one thing for sure.

Whatever I was looking for, it wasn't here.

3

A LOVE LIKE BREATHING

My head spins vertiginously, my body plummeting through empty space. In a shadowy room, a black octagonal table appears with two chairs covered in pulsating vines. Someone's breathing next to me.

Her white gown and face illuminate the entire room. Smoke from a lit cigarette weaves rotating fractal patterns into the air. Her eyes burn sapphire.

"My God, Celeste, what're you doing here?"

She drags from her cigarette, its orange glow a sinister eye in the dark. "I'm here to remind you of your purpose."

"What purpose?"

She puffs for a long time, then blows out a plume of green smoke. "Listen, Dylan, we've been together for many lifetimes."

"I know. But why was our time together in *this* life so short?"

"Because our soul's plan is to have a spiritual friendship."

"Okay, but what does that mean exactly?"

She puts out the cigarette, transferring heat from the table to me. "I know your every atom, don't you see? You're my Adam; I'm your Eve. We're a primordial couple, forged in the Furnace of Creation. We'll always be connected, even if separated by time and space, which are just illusions anyway."

She disappears for a moment, then materializes in my lap, smiling. I delight in her playfulness.

"I know. Somehow, I've always known."

She squeezes me, smelling like coconut, jasmine, and the sea. "Just remember two things—we'll always have paradise together."

"And the other?" I ask, putting my nose between the valley of her breasts.

She giggles, rubbing my head. "The second, silly, is with love, all things are possible."

Her words set off an explosion. Cathedral spires launch us into the sky, torching the atmosphere, igniting stars. Space's black skin becomes our new flesh, the constellations our open pores, numerous suns the luminous chakras of our energetic connection.

Stay close to the songs, and you'll always stay close to me.

∞

I awoke to the sound of someone's radio playing "Higher Love" from the bunk above me. A man's hairy, reddish-brown legs and black-socked feet were hanging down, swaying to the beat of the music.

How odd.

There was a smooth, round object resting in my palm. It was the green plastic egg Elsie had given me.

Thank God. It wasn't just a dream.

I shook it, listening to its contents rattling in its oblong cage. Before I could even open it, someone said, "Nah man, it's not time yet."

Slowly rising from the bed, I wondered if Radioman had said that. If he had, he wasn't even acknowledging my presence. While he harmonized with the song, I just stood there, watching him, until the song faded out.

His eyes shot open, a strong electrical field pulsing around him. "Sorry man, I really get into my music."

"I can see that," I said, chuckling. "I love music too. The name's Dylan Hunter."

He shook my hand eagerly, his palms like rare steak. "I know, man. I'm Jeremiah Bolt."

Oh my God! It's that mysterious shadow man again. What the hell?

He ran his hands through his oily black hair, winking at me with the same spark from my green-light dream. His eyes swirled in mesmerizing patterns.

"I know all about your dream," he said ominously.

"And how the hell would you know about that?"

"Because I'm part of you. I'm the one who orchestrates your dreams anyway."

There was a short pause, then "Stereo Hearts" started playing on his radio. "Are you like my inner DJ or something?"

"Well, I did lead you to your career." He nodded his head to the beat, his eyes closing again. "It's just like Celeste used to say, 'Stay close to the songs.'"

I guess this guy is inside my head.

Bolt leapt off the bed. "Get your focus off here," he said, pointing to my forehead, "and get it back here, where it belongs." He dug his index finger into my sternum, just like Celeste used to do.

I tried to step back, but I was already leaning against another bunk. "Um, yeah, well, I gotta take a shower. We can jam out when I get back."

He stared at me, still pointing at my chest. "Nah man, I'll be gone by then. But make sure you keep your eyes *wide* open."

"Why?"

"You'll see." He walked back to his black duffle bag and ~~began pulling out~~ clothes.

I couldn't get to the bathroom fast enough. But when I finally arrived at the shower stall, I paused, took a deep breath, and stepped in. Closing my eyes for a moment, I luxuriated in the hot water, trying to wash away the weirdness of the morning. Yet Bolt persisted, his voice echoing in my head: *Look down, man!*

As soon as I opened my eyes, lightning struck my heart. Someone had written something on the exposed pipe.

The words were written sideways in red paint. My heart accelerated, ascended up my throat. I felt it pulsing there rapidly, relentlessly, while I stared at the pipe.

The Source of Love is within you!

I read it again to make sure I wasn't imagining all this. Despite three readings, the words were still the same.

Keep your eyes wide open!

I jumped out of the shower, wrapped the towel around my waist, and sprinted down the corridor, which seemed a lot longer on the way back. The water was still running.

My flip-flops clattered on the concrete as I grabbed the door jam, whirled back into the room.

And just like that, Jeremiah Bolt was gone.

No sign of the radio either.

But there was a note on my bed. I wondered how Bolt had written it so fast, or if somehow, he had already written it, just for me:

My Dearest Beloved:

The day you sold your heart and happiness to someone else, you betrayed yourself. The sad truth is, you never bought it back from her, and she never offered to sell it back to you. In fact, she owns you.

Yes, of course I'm talking about Celeste, the one holding your heart hostage. Who else has enslaved your mind? But guess what? The love she gave you is . . . surprise! . . . already within you. The Garden of Eden you thought you had created with her, has in truth, been inside you all along.

YOU are the love you need—always have been, always will be. Through every heartbreak, through every heart-thrill, I have been there. I am the One who marshals you to Love, the One who orders the retreat from fear. I am your commander-in-chief, your generous general, your admiring admiral, your soul sovereign. Who needs government and laws when my rule is not with an iron fist, but a golden heart?

Who am I? I am the love you seek and will always find. I am the first resurrection, the final revelation of your soul. With me by your side, you can never lose; you can only love.

Embrace me, for you will never need another. I am Like a Lover Never Leaving. I am your Gift of Infinite Surprise.

Eternally yours,
The Advocate

The note and my towel fell to the floor. I just stood there, naked, the morning sun streaming into my searing skin.

A voice, one I was just beginning to remember, emanated from the sunlight: *Go to the meditation center tonight. There, all will be revealed!*

∞

Fearing this town was haunted with ghosts—both real and imagined—I decided to get the hell out of here. Bolt's letter and that luminous voice be damned.

There was still frost on my car's front windshield, and ice particles sparkled in the bright sunshine, danced in front of my eyes, then converged into a blinding flash.

It felt like staring directly into the sun.

I put my hands up to protect my eyes, but when I looked again, the effect was gone—the particles were stationary.

What in the world is going on here?

Feeling the urge to investigate, I zipped my jacket up to my neck and turned into the street. Though it was cold, I relished the warm sun on my face, the light sting in my lungs. After a few minutes, I came upon a window with a bright yellow sign advertising for a meditation session at seven tonight.

Wait, no, it couldn't be.

That mediation class was at the Kootenay Shambhala Centre, the same place I'd found online while staying at Celeste's house. Was it just a coincidence, or was it a true moment of synchronicity? Either way, I felt compelled. I had to check it out.

But my phone was telling me it was only 11:33. I still had over seven hours. What could I do until then?

For now, I needed to find a place to eat. I walked down Baker Street until I stumbled upon this place called the Full Circle Café. At first, I just scanned the menu through the window, but then I noticed a quote from John Milton's *Paradise Lost*: "The mind is its own place, and in itself can make a Heaven of Hell, a Hell of Heaven."

Goddamn, whatever I was on, I hoped it would wear off soon; I couldn't take much more of this unsolicited, non-human advice. As I stepped into the café, a bell rang above the door, and when I peered in, it was packed with customers. *What a relief.* It would make the perfect hiding place from this morning's madness.

∞

After an exhausting two-hour trek through the streets of Nelson to contemplate Celeste's offer of fatherhood and spiritual friendship—followed by a long afternoon nap to forget all about it—I arrived at the meditation center just before 7:00 p.m. On my trip up the staircase to the third floor, I felt like I was ascending a ladder into the unknown. I really didn't know why I was here, or what to expect.

Once in the Main Shrine Room, I sat down on a red meditation cushion with a yellow bullseye, watching the incense swirl to the ceiling. Some of the light from the street poured through the windows, shining on a golden Buddha, who was perched on a large table and was gleaming, almost grinning. A bald man in a saffron robe struck a gong, its reverberations grounding me in the now.

I looked absently out the window, visions of Celeste coming unbidden.

∞

The room morphs into a prison. I'm trapped inside.

Celeste smiles, standing outside the jail cell, twirling a ring of keys on an elastic string. The key ring orbits faster and faster around the nucleus of her hand, its string stretching, yo-yoing between the metal bars. She's teasing me.

Just as I'm ready to say something, the string snaps, keys hurtling toward me like a hammer throw. I catch them right before they impale my eyes. I want to reprimand her for being so careless, but she's already gone.

The keys shimmer with gold-green light. I can't stop staring at them.

Bolt's voice pings off each bar of the cell. *Celeste is not the warden. You are!*

My deep laughter shatters the prison bars, strands of human cells swimming out of their broken pieces. I hopscotch from one nucleus to the next, drop into one of their miniature oceans—and rafting on mitochondria—drift toward an infinite horizon.

Intense moonlight reflects on the ocean's surface, celestial melodies flowing into my mouth, moving in rhythm with the rolling waves. Starlight points flash from the water to my eyes, streaming through my pupils like threaded needles. Soon, the particles coalesce into a pair of hands, holding me firmly in a divine embrace.

I am the vine and you are the branches.

The light grows brighter and brighter, pulsating like a cosmic orgasm. "Who's there?"

Don't you know who I am?

"I can't even see you."

I am the woman behind the mask.

"Oh God, won't this trip ever end?"

My Dear Dylan, don't you know? Spirit is the ultimate trip. You don't need drugs to take you there.

A woman in a golden robe condenses out of the light. The mask is there for a moment, but quickly dissolves. Her face alchemizes into Celeste.

I am Andalucía, she who walks in the light. I am your guide.

"Guide for what?"

Your journey to find the Ultimate Love. To discover the One who will finally answer the longings of your heart. Caps ?

"You mean Celeste?"

No, Dylie! You have to let her go. Besides, isn't it time to stop giving your power away to others? Isn't it time to redeem your Eden within?

She laughs gently, like little waves lapping on the shore of a lake. Her aura expands, fills all the empty spaces within me. Then a primordial memory takes over, launching me into the sky.

∞

Beethoven's *Moonlight Sonata* propels my flight through the clouds—piano notes swirling around the wind—its haunting melody deepened by shadow, yet tinged with sparks of light.

I am elemental atom, music orbiting around me in electron storms—where vibrations fast, then slow— solidify me into a body again. As I descend, waves crash lightly onto the shore, while a cool breeze caresses my face, whips my hair.

I open my eyes. It's early morning, just before dawn.

The only light is the full moon, radiating over my body and the beach, its glow reflected on the vast mirror of the ocean.

Is this real?

As if to answer my question, the wind picks up, swirling sand stinging my eyes, my hands too late to cover them. But soon, my tears begin to wash away those rough crystals, and it isn't long until I see them glinting in the moonlight.

To see the universe in a grain of sand!

I look around for the source of the voice, but no one's there. I'm all alone.

Longing strikes like lightning. I cough several times, my heart beating hard and fast in my chest. A powerful yet gentle force twirls me in the breeze, and I dance on the packed sand till I get dizzy. I fall down and giggle, making sand angels until my arms and legs burn.

When I finally stand up, my white shirt and pants illuminate my left ring finger, which has a circular, grooved outline around it. Shouldn't there be a wedding band there?

Right on cue, Celeste appears, her blue eyes piercing the fog. She whispers in my ear, "I'm sorry."

I try to embrace her, but she's only mist. A light shines from her lunar plexus, temporarily blinding me. Echoes of her kisses and touches ripple in the rivers of my blood, and she's inside me again, though light years away, locked in some inner dimension. I cry out for her.

But just like always, my cries of longing are in vain.

I feel her absence profoundly, almost more than her presence. The heaving in my chest travels south to my stomach, and I retch into the water several times.

If this is all I have to look forward to, then I want to die.

Don't worry, I will save you, a reassuring, peaceful voice says. A green light flashes, surrounding me in a radiant bubble, outshining the moon.

"Who are you?"

Don't be afraid, my Child. I will lead you to a love affair that never ends.

"Are you God?"

He answers in music: "Moonlight Sonata" fades out; "Amazing Grace" floods in. His smile flows out of the green light, emitting a knowing laugh in my heart.

I am your Advocate, here to take you on a journey, to show you the true nature of Love. For Love is the reason, the purpose, the only reality. Just follow the music of my voice.

The song shifts again from "Amazing Grace" to *Adagio for Strings*, building toward its intense climax. Escalating strings rush through my veins like sonic champagne.

In this moment, I realize The Advocate is divinity personified, the source of all love. When I connect to Him, I'm free. I don't need anyone else to feel loved.

Are you ready?

Before I can even answer, my body begins to lift, floating toward a churning hurricane. I try to resist, but its pull is like a black hole. The Advocate puts his hand on my arm, quieting the storm of my thoughts.

You must rest within your resistance.

As we approach the eye of the cyclone, the atoms of my body vibrate faster and faster.

"Are we headed toward annihilation?"

No my Child. We are heading toward its opposite: At-one-ment.

He takes my left hand, golden light flashing, pulsing around my ring finger. We sing and rejoice, flying into the vortex together.

∞

Never-ending fields of undulating indigo surround me in a sentient ocean, where each wave is alive, intelligent, somehow allowing me to breathe.

Bioluminescent fish race past me in flashes of green and pink and orange and yellow, performing acrobatics like underwater airplanes. They synchronize as the Kabbalah Tree of Life, then dissipate into bubbles, forming intricate chains of Ohm symbols.

I am the Alpha and the Omega.

My God, what is this place?

The fish lift me out of the water, propping me up in front of a stormy sky. Despite the cold air, a subtle, warm glow permeates my body.

Silver-blue clouds spin faster and faster, propelling the fish into the distant horizon, where they burst like fireworks, colorful streaks streaming from the sky.

I can't tell if I'm laughing or crying, coming or going, dreaming or dying.

My dear Dylan, such distinctions no longer matter, for you have arrived at the Divine Intersection.

A white-orange orb at the eye of the storm pulls me toward it like a tractor beam. Every electron in my body sizzles through empty space—firecrackering—seeding the clouds with firefly light.

Behold, for YOU are that light. Now is the time to see yourself as a Bright Sun, as a Beautiful Song of God!

Once everything washes white, I surrender completely.

∞

My eyes adjust to the whitewash of light, waves flowing through prisms of shifting color. The walls appear organic—expanding and contracting with my breath—as my hands phase in and out, straddling multiple planes of existence. It feels like I'm still tripping.

"What is this, some kind of rainbow room?"

I look around for The Advocate, but I can only sense his voice animating the space around me.

You are in the anteroom.

"A what?"

As you would understand, a waiting room of sorts.

"Oh, you mean like purgatory?"

No, you're not being punished. You're being held until it's your turn.

"Turn? Turn for what? Why are you speaking in riddles?"

Everything is a riddle to a closed mind.

The Advocate laughs warmly and gently, then a star of bluish-white light shimmers—growing from the center like a slowly opening mouth.

Come to the light, my friend. You are safe here.

"So . . . am I dead or what?"

Death does not exist in this realm. Here, you are eternally alive.

The room glows green, pulsing in spikes of gold. *Come! Your appointment with eternity has arrived.*

∞

I walk through a luminous doorway into a room made of crystalline marble. Electric blue veins course through it, flashing like lightning, pulsing in time with my heart. Geometric shapes flow out of the walls, then swirl and coalesce into a courtroom full of gleaming white furniture. Men and women in a jury box all wear black, offsetting their pale, blank faces, their eyes hypnotized by the patterns still spinning on the walls.

right

Two counselors stand by their desks. The one on the ~~left~~ right wears a white, flowing robe composed of light, that same spiral pattern emanating from him. His skin is the most radiant I've ever seen, his smile the warmest I've ever felt.

I am your Advocate. I will release you from the tyranny of your self-loathing.

As soon as I sit down, a sharp pang stabs my gut. My opposing counsel looks like he's been forged in the flames of Hell. He's wearing a black suit, as if dressed for a funeral, and his hair is bright crimson, spiked into long nails. On his black tie is a red dragon, its massive wings like a sinister sunrise, fire breathing out of the tip. His beady golden eyes bore through me, igniting a wildfire within.

I turn to The Advocate. "Is that me?"

He is the unhealed part of you. We must overcome his negativity before you can begin your spiritual adventure in earnest.

"And how do we do that?"

With the weapon of Love. It is more powerful than atom bombs; it is what fuels the stars; it is what keeps the dance of creation going.

"And you're sure it'll work?"

My Holy Friend, it has never failed.

"I wish I shared your confidence."

At the judge's bench, a blank movie screen rolls down, images of that spiral pattern projected there. His face slowly fades into view. I recognize him immediately.

The judge appears as an older, fiercer version of me. He has slick black hair, a trimmed beard peppered with gray, and ears like satellite dishes. His tie is decorated with hurricanes and galaxies, tornados and tsunami. Nostrils flaring, he stares at me with icy blue eyes.

"I'm my own judge? That doesn't make any sense."

"You will refer to me as Judge Storm, Mr. Dragon."

"The name's Dylan, your honor."

"But your spirit is a dragon. Why would I refer to you otherwise?"

"Look, if I'm dead, just send me wherever I'm supposed to go, or if I'm alive, just take me back home. I'm tired of this."

"That's the problem with you humans. You're so dualistic."

"HA! And what are you, some kind of alien?"

"I am the one you have alienated, yes."

"Jesus, why does everyone speak in riddles around here?"

I've already told you, you polarize everything. The universe of understanding lies in between.

"See, what does that even mean?"

By the end of this trial, you will understand everything.

"Trial? What am I even being accused of?"

"You don't know?" Judge Storm thunders.

"How should I know? I haven't understood anything that's been going on since I got here . . . wherever here is."

"Well, Mr. Dragon, ever since Celeste left, you've sentenced yourself to life without love. How do you plead?"

"What? When did I do this? Whatever you're smoking your honor, I want some." Judge Storm rolls his eyes.

He pleads innocent, your honor. Guilt is no match against the arsenal of Love.

"But first, I must show your client something. It's something he must understand before the proceedings can begin."

The Advocate's eyes expand to fill up the room. I don't know what's going to happen, but I know it's not going to be good.

∞

Fierce winds turn rain into bullets, whipping through trees and blowing roofs off houses; cascading waves crash into piers, capsizing boats; tornados whirl on the beach and rip through the streets, sucking up everything in their path; jagged lightning strikes power lines, orange and yellow sparks shooting through the air.

I want to run, but there's nowhere to hide.

My heart pounds like a prisoner clamoring for freedom from his ribcage, right before the claws of the storm pull me in. It tosses me from one side of the street to the other, trees and telephone poles falling all around me.

If I weren't dead before, I might die now.

I take cover under a roof, but when it flies away, I cover my head with my arms, debris raining down.

This is it. I know I'm doomed.

This is your internal state. You must heal this first.

"I don't understand. How am I like a storm?"

Your judge is a storm. What other evidence do you need?

"Here we go with the stupid riddles again."

My friend, the storm IS the riddle. ridiculous

One of the tornados bears down on me, so I sprint toward the beach, aiming for the flat, wet part of the sand. Tidal waves swell and break onto the shore, yearning to pull me into the water. I might escape one or the other, but not both.

Do I want to drown, or be sucked into the sky?

I don't even have time to decide. The tornado scoops me up, spins me around toward the dark clouds. Exhausted, I let my body go limp.

Right before blacking out, The Advocate says, *Reason cannot solve the riddle. Only Love can.*

∞

Judge Storm returns to the screen, staring at me like I'm a complete idiot. "Well?"

Once I realize I'm still alive, I stare right back. I'm tired of playing these stupid games. "Well, what?"

"How do you plead?"

"Guilty. I'm obviously not worthy of existence, so just go ahead and kill me. I deserve to die."

"But you've already died, Mr. Dragon. What else can we do?"

"Do you have a prison you can throw me in?"

"And if I do, how long should I sentence you?"

"Forever. It's what I deserve."

"My my, perhaps *you* should be the judge here."

I glare at him, feeling like that storm I barely escaped. "Why are you laughing? This isn't funny."

He smirks, mimicking my expression. "You're right, Mr. Dragon, self-condemnation is *never* funny. But shame and blame are not your name."

"Huh? Come again?"

"We don't believe in punishment here. We consider it a form of violence. Besides, Love is the most effective teacher." He grins enigmatically. "So . . . we're going to give you what you've always wanted."

I chuckle. "Wow, I didn't even know that was an option."

His eyes darken, his smile deepens. "It's not what you think, Mr. Dragon. In order to get what your soul truly desires, you're going to have to give up what your ego has always wanted. Do you think you're up to the challenge?"

"Do I even have a choice?"

"Of course, you always have a choice, but your soul's already made the decision. It's just waiting for you to catch up."

"Wait, how is that even possible?"

Judge Storm laughs again. "That's one of life's many paradoxes, Mr. Dragon. But don't worry. One of my emissaries will show you the way."

∞

All is blackness. Water rushes around me, pushing me down a long, steeply descending chute, and it feels like I'm riding a pipeline straight to Hell. I wait for the water to get scalding hot.

But it gets progressively colder.

There's a sliver of light below. An intense pressure launches me into the air, and I land with a splash onto a wet, metal floor that smells of rust and sulfur. I shoot up to a standing position, wiping my hands on my pants. "Ew, yuck, how did I get into a sewer?"

No answer.

When I look up, droplets land on my forehead like some kind of water torture. That crescent of light is brighter now, providing enough light to see the subtle outlines of objects. As water streams into the river at my feet, I realize there's no turning back.

Nowhere to go but forward.

I call to the ceiling: "This doesn't look like the courtroom. Aren't I supposed to receive my judgment and sentence?"

Just keep walking. Someone familiar will show you the way.

There's a blinding flash of light, then the golden outline of a figure. "Who's there?"

He walks toward me holding a torch. Like flipping a switch, everything's illuminated. "Herrrrrrrrrrrrrrrrre's Johnny!" he announces, somehow mimicking both Ed McMahon's and Jack Nicholson's voices at the same time.

"Oh my God, Bolt. Is that you?"

"Who else could make an entrance like this, man?"

This is the first close-up I've gotten of his face. He looks like Cesar Milan from *The Dog Whisperer.*

I chuckle. "Is there a dog that needs to be rehabilitated?"

"Hey man, this is the form *you* picked, not me." He points toward the shadows. "Come on, follow me!"

I fall into stride behind him, water splashing around our feet. Somehow, the sound of a faucet dripping is constantly in earshot—never softer, never louder. "So . . . where are we headed, then?"

"I think it's best you don't know. I wouldn't want to spoil the surprise."

"You know I hate surprises. Can't you just give me a little hint?"

Eddie Money's "Two Tickets to Paradise" blares through my head, water drops speeding up to match the song's tempo. "That seems promising."

"Promising doesn't even *begin* to describe this place. It'll blow your mind."

As we trek further, that sliver of light grows in intensity, like a half moon waxing to full. "Okay, we're here," he says confidently.

"Really? This is it?"

"Nah man, it's down there. Go ahead. Press your ear against the grate."

I see only light, so I turn my ear to listen. First it's silent, then I hear the most intricate birdsong ever. The notes seem random, but after a few moments, the birds begin singing "Ode to Joy," the final movement of The Ninth Symphony.

"Oh my God."

"Nah man, it's just Beethoven," he snickers.

"That's not funny, man. What is this place?"

"Only one way to find out."

Cackling, he disappears in a blue-white flash. His torch falls into the water, extinguishing itself.

The sound of rushing water roars into my ears. The grate blows open, leaving the porthole exposed. "Oh no, this ain't gonna be good."

Relax! Just let the current guide you.

"Easy for you to say!" The water soon overtakes me, blasting me through the open porthole. I watch myself— in slow motion—cascading toward a large grove of trees.

Talk about a leap of faith.

As I hurtle toward the ground, Bolt sings U2's "Vertigo," piping it directly into the temporal lobe of my brain.

If I weren't about to plummet to my death, I might've laughed. Some instinct takes over, and I grab one of the tree branches, slow my momentum, swing off it like a monkey, flip several times in the air, and finally land on the ground, planting perfectly.

Apparently, in this place, I can defy the laws of physics. If those laws even have any meaning here.

I stand on the periphery of a dense, green jungle. Beyond the canopy of trees, an ice-capped mountain shoots up into the cloudy horizon, piercing the rain clouds. At first, all I hear are crows and cicadas, but when I listen closer, I notice something rustling in the leaves. My breathing catches in my throat, my blood whistles through my ears. I try to remain quiet.

"Who's there?"

Emerging from the gate of the forest is that dragon guy from the courtroom. "We're more alike than you think."

His hair emits an electrical current like a Tesla coil, and his eyes flash yellow caution signals. Though we look similar, he appears much taller, much more imposing.

"You're in the Jungle of true perception. Here, you see everything as it *really* is."

"And what's your name?"

"Just call me Drake."

As he walks closer, his skin becomes translucent and reflective, just like my own. Our faces perform a frightening dance of imitation.

"Drake, stop playing tricks on me. Why am I being punished?"

A light rain begins to mist across the trees, thunder rumbling in the distance.

"You still don't get it, do you? You've been punishing yourself this whole time."

"God Almighty, why does everyone give me evasive answers around here?"

"Because you're not willing to face the truth yet."

"And what truth would that be?"

He shakes his head, chuckling. "That this place is both Hell and Heaven, all wrapped up into one. You choose which side to inhabit."

"Okay, once again, you've lost me."

"Well, that's no surprise. You're always lost."

He closes the gap between us, staring deeply into my eyes. At first his irises swirl like everything from that weird courtroom, but after a few seconds, the spinning stops. His pupils dilate, and soon, I see a perfect reflection of myself. An aura of golden light shimmers around his body.

"This is how others see you," he says, in perfect imitation of The Advocate.

His aura soon disappears, everything around me darkening like a solar eclipse. My face looks panic-stricken. "Now, this is how you see yourself."

Drake's eyes turn to storms, right before he transforms into a giant grizzly bear. My mind screams to run, but I just stand there, too paralyzed to move. His large, furry arm swats at my head, razor claws slicing into my throat. I fall to the muddy ground, warm blood oozing from my neck and chest. The bear collapses on top of me.

Just because this place is beautiful . . . doesn't mean it isn't dangerous!

∞

Before I can even ask for help, the attack is over. Drake is gone.

I run my hands along my neck, but there's no blood, not even a scratch. I just feel fiercer, more alive.

In front of me now is a marble fountain with a cracked bowl and weathered concrete base. Prismatic waters arc into the sky, soaking the trees, changing the color of their leaves. On both sides of this fountain stand two moss-covered granite statues—one a panther, the other a pterodactyl. Every time I look away, they move; but when I stare straight at them, they remain still.

The sun streams through the foliage, growing progressively brighter, almost screaming, until a high-pitched whine expands like cicadas patched through an amplifier. I cover my ears and clamp my eyes closed, praying the sound will stop.

But it gets worse. It pulses inside my head, creating incredible pressure, inflating my skull like a balloon. *If you're going to kill me, please do it now!*

When the sound implodes, the pain evaporates. The panther statue animates, slinks toward me. I remember my scuffle with Drake and want to run, but some invisible force field holds me in place. My mind sprints in circles.

"Whoever you are, please don't hurt me. I've been through enough."

I would agree with that. The panther creeps closer. He's decked out like a rainbow zebra, his stripes rippling with shifting color.

"Are you The Advocate in different form?"

Not exactly, but close enough.

"Are you going to kill me?"

Approach me. I won't harm you.

"I can't. I'm stuck somehow."

Release yourself from your fear, and you will be ~~able to move.~~ free

I take a few deep breaths, thinking of Elsie. Suddenly, she appears, riding on the back of the smiling panther. I want to hug her, but I'm still frozen.

"Oh my God, Elsie, what are you doing here? I thought you were still in Nelson."

"I am."

"Wait . . . so you're in two places at once?"

"Sure, why not?"

"Well, I guess nothing else makes any sense around here, so why should that?"

Here, we follow quantum laws. Everything is nonlocal, so it's possible to be in two places at once.

Something inside me unlocks. I step forward to only an arm's length from the panther, and a will not my own compels me to reach out, pet the feline on his head. He purrs like a house cat.

Make sure to keep your attention, for I will bite if you lose focus. The panther nips at my fingers, and I retract them. Elsie giggles.

"So what should I call you? Just Panther?"

I don't have a name per se, but I am He Who Hunts Down Meaning in Dreams. If you see me when you sleep, it's a good omen.

"So you're saying this is a dream?"

In a manner of speaking, yes.

"Then I should be able to figure out what's going on, right?"

The prey of meaning has not offered its neck yet.

"I don't understand."

In time, you will.

The panther vanishes in a flash, taking Elsie with him.

"No, bring her back!" I try to run after her, but I'm paralyzed again.

It's too late; she's already gone. In her place, the sound of gigantic flapping wings fills my ears.

∞

The statue of the pterodactyl breathes to life. He flies over to me with bellows-like wings, which kick up dust from the ground, blinding me temporarily. When the flapping stops, the majestic pterosaur stands statuesque, five feet in front of me, eerily quiet. His irises are a rich amber color, like peering into the past.

"Who are you?" I ask.

He screeches while remaining still, staring ~~right~~ *straight* through me.

"I'm sorry, I don't speak your language."

Use your mind to speak!

"Oh right, I keep forgetting."

I represent primal truth. I am the one who screams in your ears when you refuse to listen.

Something suddenly looks familiar in those ancient eyes. "Oh yeah, I think you've been in my dreams before."

I am in everyone's dreams, in some prehistoric form or another. Do you remember my message to you?

"I wish, but I haven't remembered anything since I got here. Wherever here is."

Message to this:

~~He opens his mouth, screeching.~~ *You are not made of reptiles. You are made of angels!*

There's a glimmer of understanding, but it fizzles out before I can grasp it. I don't know what to say, so I just ~~stare~~ *gaze* at him, admiring his wings.

Your rational mind is a roadblock on the highway of spiritual understanding. You must leap over that before you can accept the truth of who you are.

"And who is that, exactly?"

That's for you to figure out. But you must go deeper to feel the eternal *within* ~~you~~

He shrinks to the size of a hummingbird, then bullets into me, and somehow, I am able to absorb this miniature pterodactyl without pain. He expands with each flap of his wings, merging with my lungs. My heart becomes the head of this magnificent beast, his timeless eyes flickering open.

able

I'm soaring over the canopy of trees, slicing through the clouds, setting the horizon on fire. "Are we flying into the sun?"

No dear Icarus, not today. We are flying toward your own inner illumination.

"Will I die?"

Only what no longer serves you will die. You are safe.

My third eye opens, new fields of vision expanding in front of me. As I glide through the air, everything is bathed in a golden glaze of honey.

Now that you are seeing with your heart, everything will be infused with magic.

"I've never felt so ecstatic. Is this how God sees?"

You are wearing the goggles of your Divine Vision. You will need them now, more than ever, before you meet her.

Lightning bolts zap around me. "Uh oh, who's that?"

You know her already, intimately. She is the one who has promised to answer the longings of your heart.

I know exactly who she is. Laughing, I accelerate into the skyfire, fusing with the sun.

∞

descend to the ground.

Light explodes, scattering in a trillion points, shooting stars streaking across the sky. Large willow trees, illuminated in fiberoptic blue, provide a soft glow for a path slowly unraveling in front of me. In this magical place, I sense a sentient intelligence infusing everything.

Welcome to the Inner Cosmos, Dylie. It's your true home!

Andalucía's form fades in slowly—first her golden gown appears, followed by her long eyelashes, fluttering like butterfly wings; then her eyes, hair, and dolphin earrings flow through the full spectrum of color; and the coup de grace is her oval, opal face, flipping like a slide projector from Celeste to Julie to Marina and back to Andalucía again. I can't keep anything straight about her from one moment to the next.

Does my appearance mystify you?

"Everything here mystifies me."

She giggles mellifluously. *Good! A sense of wonder and an appreciation for life's mystery are great places to start.*

"Yeah, but I feel like I'm moving in circles."

Well, stop being so linear then!

When she reaches out for my hands, her touch is so warm, so intimate, like making love with just our fingers, passing ecstasy back and forth in a lover's game of tennis. If this is what holding hands feels like, I wonder how a kiss would feel. Or more.

Would you like to find out?

Andalucía morphs into Celeste, wearing a purple winter coat, yellow scarf, and white stocking cap. With her luminous smile broadcasting her attraction for me, she is unbearably cute.

Snow slowly falls, and I stand transfixed by the shimmering lights from what appears to be Spokane— only much brighter—punctuated by flashing red towers. Her glacier eyes stare right through me.

She grabs my coat, bunching it with her fists. *I want you. Just surrender.*

"But I don't want to. You'll hurt me again."

But I am not she. Look closer. I am the Lover Who Will Never Leave You.

"Why are you doing this to me?"

My dear Dylan, this is the image you wanted lifted up to Love's Altar.

She cups my cheek, just like Celeste used to do, as our lips become electrodes, shocking my soul from my body.

Don't you see? I am the one who came shining through both of you as you connected to that ecstatic electricity. It was a time when you surrendered to Love. Besides, you should be grateful. Some people live their entire lives and never experience such beauty, such profound connection.

"But I want to experience that again."

Don't worry, you will. Just follow me. I'll show you the way.

We soar into the sky, her golden aura eclipsing the full moon.

∞

All the moonlight condenses into Andalucía's gown. She smiles, placing her palm over my heart, jolting me.

She's Celeste again.

We melt together. Submerging into her body, I flow to the rhythm of her heart, her breath. I'm back in the womb, ready to be born again.

Her cells weave into mine, interpenetrating our pores, warm chills surging and cresting, my atoms disintegrating, exploding like firecrackers. In this electric ocean, I surf from one wave to the next, trying to stop them from crashing. But their course is inexorable.

Don't fight this, Dylan. Let go! Love is ego annihilation, then fusion with the Divine.

Shooting down a winding chute, I fall seemingly forever—until I land on the hearth of a crystalline cabin. Water downpours all over the translucent floor, extinguishing a marble fireplace with several hisses, and then everything goes dark. When I feel a hand touch my chest, I recoil.

Relax Dylan, it's just me.

"Celeste or Andalucía?"

What a silly question. We're one and the same.

Our bodies hum, illuminating the space expanding around us. Her turquoise robe floats like a raft in tropical water. The room dissolves, ice walls melting, seagulls calling, waves rolling onto the shore. The sun shines warm on my face, the breeze blows cool on my skin.

Let me show you a love easy and natural, like breathing. When you inhale, you receive love; when you exhale, you give love. You see, Love is Spiritual Oxygen.

Our breath syncs with the ocean, scintillating salt notes hanging in the air.

∞

We follow the shoreline extending into eternity. The ocean water is aquamarine close to the beach, ultramarine farther out, just like Andalucía's eyes, and her sunrise smile is a symphonic broadcast. I put my arm around her shoulders, pulling her close.

I know I can communicate telepathically, but I want to speak aloud so my thoughts sound real. "So, are you like, Aphrodite or something?"

She laughs like the waves lapping on the shore. *That's one of my many names, and perhaps a fitting one for this location. I am born of the sea; its foam is my essence.*

"But this is all in my head, right? None of this is real."

It's as real as you believe it to be, Dylan. But let me ask you this: How do you know this *isn't reality?*

"I guess I don't."

And how do you know your waking life isn't a dream?

"I don't. But that seems pretty farfetched."

Remember the message from The Advocate: *"Love is the only reality." Everything else is an illusion.*

"So, what you're saying is, without Love, life is meaningless."

She winks, kisses me. The energy field around us intensifies—shimmering, vibrating, singing.

"Why can't it always be like this?"

Because human love is imperfect. What you're experiencing now is a slice of perfect, divine love.

"Wait . . . a slice? So there's more?"

Of course. Love grows exponentially. Its nature is to expand and color the palette of Infinity.

"So you mean it keeps getting bigger and better?"

She giggles like a young girl. *What else would evolution be for?*

My heart leaps upon seeing Elysia again. I scoop her up, swing her around, our laughter piggybacking on the wind. Tears stream down our cheeks.

We spin and spin, never getting dizzy. I want to be on this merry-go-round with her forever.

But eventually, our momentum slows down. I set her delicately on the sand, kneel in front of her so we're at eye level. "We'll be together again," I say. "I promise."

Don't worry, Daddy. Even if time and space keep us apart, Love is forever.

She kisses my forehead, sprints toward the ocean, and I chase after her, diving deep into the water.

Swimming above me, she freestyles with ease, periodically turning her head to breathe. On her pink bathing suit, the name ELYSIA is spelled in sparkling rhinestones, outshining the sun. Her thick goggles amplify her blue eyes, and her smile cannot be contained, as if being in water were the happiest state in the universe.

She pinches her nose, corkscrews downward—riding the stream of a narrow vortex—until we're side by side. Somehow, in this place, we don't need to come up for air.

We hold hands and kick slowly ahead, exploring the limitless blue.

∞

A large plug pops, abruptly ending our journey through this aquatic universe. As Elysia and I spiral down a vortex to the ocean floor, a door opens in the sand below us, and she spins through the opening, bubbles of her laughter floating back to my face. I follow her through an airlock, then into a dark, dry room, where the only sound is her giggling.

"Come on, Daddy, turn on the lights."

"How, Elsie? I don't see a switch."

"Use your mind, silly."

I concentrate hard, imagining the brightest bulb I can think of. Light slowly expands into the room. "Hey, I did it."

"I knew you could, Daddy. Come on, follow me," she says, as we pass easily through a membranous wall.

Inside is a pulsing geode, diamonds flashing from an unknown light source. In the center stand four pillars made of blue marble, and on top sits a large gemstone, rotating on an invisible axis, exploding with rainbow color. *the voice of the Advocate spilling out.*

This is the radiant inner jewel that holds everything divine in its facets—Joy, Ecstasy, Love, and your Eternal Innocence. It can never be damaged by anyone or anything. It is your internal treasure, the essence of embracing the Lover Never Leaving.

"Can I have the jewel?" Elysia asks. "It's so beautiful."

The Advocate materializes into the room, smiling, pointing to her chest. *You already have it, right here.*

"Really? I don't see it."

167

His hands flash, and a smaller version of the jewel falls into her palms. It's bright purple with swirls of pink. Her mouth drops open, her eyes full moons. "Wow, cool! How'd you do that?"

Anything is possible in this realm.

"Awesome! What other tricks can you do?"

The Advocate laughs, sparks of light emanating from his mouth. She jumps on these miniature stars, playing hopscotch from one to the other.

There. That should keep her busy for a while.

"Wow, you make everything look so easy."

All it takes is a playful state of mind, and a willingness to believe in magic again.

"Can't I just stay here forever? I would be supremely happy that way."

Wouldn't we all? No, your adventure isn't over yet. But always remember this: the Adventure of Love lasts a lifetime.

Coldplay's "Adventure of a Lifetime" emanates from the jewel's facets, spinning the room like a record, creating tracers of light. That song is now the epicenter of the vortex, weaving a web, pulling me in.

"Oh no, not again!" I cry out.

The Advocate and Elysia waltz on the starlight, twirling toward a door at the top of the ceiling. "Hey, where are you guys going?"

We have a play date on the Eternal Playground.

"Can I join you?"

Elysia turns back to me, giggling. "Of course, silly. It was your idea in the first place."

"What? I don't remember having that idea. Are you sure?"

Their laughter accelerates the spinning of the vortex. What could I do but follow them?

As I get smaller in size, I shrink in time. I know it won't be long until I become Elysia's age—that magical age when Celeste and I first met—when we first talked about dreams. ~~on the school playground~~

∞

"Do you like dreams?" Celeste blurts out, ~~as we sit together on one of the playground popularity benches, the Eternal Playground.~~

"Yeah, dreams are cool," I say.

"Then tell me one of yours. None of my friends like talking about them. They think I'm so weird."

"Really? Well, maybe they're weird."

She leans in and smiles, her look seemingly more mature than her kid face can express. "Exactly! See, I knew you were a smart boy."

She squeezes my thigh right above my knee, like it's a groove just for her hand, and I swallow hard, desperately trying to think of a dream she'll like. When the breeze picks up, I can smell the chocolate blowing downwind from the Hershey factory. That familiar aroma reminds me of a dream.

"Ooh, I got one!"

She studies my face, giggling. "You're funny! Go on!"

"It's kinda funny and scary at the same time. I don't know if you'll like it."

"Those are the best kind! Come on, Dylie . . . I can call you Dylie, right?"

The skin at the top of her upturned nose crinkles like a bunny. With a cute face like that, I'd let her call me anything. "Sure, that's cool."

Her aquamarine eyes remind me of swimming in the sea. For a mini-eternity, I'm drowning, wondering if I'll ever come up for air.

Her long, elegant fingers reach out to save me. "Well Dylie, don't leave me hangin'! Tell me already."

I gulp loudly. "Well, I was walking downstairs after getting up one morning. When I looked out the window, I saw wolves peering in with their beady eyes, sticking their tongues out at me." She's giggling again. "What's so funny?"

"What *isn't* funny about that?"

I stick my tongue out at her, just like the wolves, and she howls with laughter, smacking the seat of the bench. I know I have her right where I want her.

"I was a little scared, but I wanted to check it out. So I walked outside to see what was going on. But it was too late. They were gone. I went around the side of the house to the clothesline, and the wolves had hung Kit-Kats on it. That's when I woke up."

She looks at me like she's had the same dream before. "See, they were nice wolves. They just wanted to leave you candy."

"Yeah, I guess. So tell me one of yours."

"Well . . . I don't know if you'll believe me. It's kinda crazy."

"So? It's a dream. It's *supposed* to be crazy."

"Okay, so . . . *this* is the dream."

"Wait, what? I don't get it."

She rubs my shoulder. "I dreamed me and you were talking about dreams. Right here. On this bench. Next to these trees." She points to the pines above us, and I imagine their needles injecting us with a powerful narcotic, obliviating us from the real world.

"Wait. Are you messing with me?"

"I wouldn't dream of it, Dylie. But that's why I like talking about dreams. A bunch of mine come true."

"Whoa, cool. Is that like, one of your superpowers?"

Her face lights up. In a weird slow-motion effect, some golden leaves fall from the oak nearby, swirl around her blonde hair for a second, then blow away.

Is all of this a dream? It just doesn't seem real.

"I guess you could call it that."

A red rubber ball rolls over to our bench. Then a skinny boy with black hair, jean shorts, and an Evanescence T-shirt yells out, "Hey kid, little help!"

I kick the ball back, right into his open hands. "Hey kid, you're pretty good. Wanna join our team?"

I want to say no, but Celeste says, "You go ahead."

"I don't have to. I can stay here with you."

She shakes her head. "No, you go ahead. Boys need to get the wolf out of them anyway." She winks.

"Well, we can be on the same team then."

Her eyebrows pop up as she points to her clothes. "Does it look like I'm dressed for kickball?"

I stare at her jade green sweater, and lilac plaid skirt, her perfect nylons and slipper shoes. "No, I guess not."

"Besides, we can talk more tomorrow. Same time?"

"Sure."

"Okay, have fun Dylie!" She waves enthusiastically.

As I sprint toward the courtyard, I look back at Celeste. She's stopped smiling. She pulls on the chain of her necklace, caresses her gold heart pendant at the center. I don't know how, or why, but I feel the same tugging at my own chest.

In that moment, I know. We'll always be connected.

∞

That connection flows into me now—filling me with love—as I venture into a sentient cave, large stalactites hanging down like dinosaur teeth. A green glow suffuses everything, turning the surrounding pools of water a deep turquoise, while yellow lights illuminate my way along the narrow trail of rock, prodding me to explore further.

"Dylie, come find us!" Celeste and Elysia call out.

"So we're playing hide and seek, eh?"

"Come on, hurry up!"

I follow the long, winding path as it grows narrower, until I arrive at a passageway I have to crawl through. Looking around for a moment, I don't see any other alternatives.

"Come on Dylie, stop wasting time. We're out here!"

I climb into the tunnel and feel the cold, wet rock underneath my hands. It's dark and seems to go on forever. Seeing no light to lead the way, I stop, my tears coming unbidden.

What's wrong, my child? The Advocate's voice rings out, echoing in my head and the tunnel, which seem to be the same thing.

"I'm so tired. I just wanna go home."

Hang in there, Dylan. We're almost finished.

"But I wanna go home. NOW!"

My dear Dylan, this IS your true home.

Wiping the tears from my cheeks, I resume crawling through the dark. After what seems like forever, something shimmers in the distance, and I am finally able to stand. Celeste and Elysia call for me again, and as their voices get louder, the light becomes brighter. I sprint toward them.

When I emerge from the cave, golden light floods my vision. Suddenly I'm a child again, blades of fluorescent grass tonguing through the cracks in my toes.

"Dylie, come in and swim with us. The water's perfect!"

I peer through a grove of palm trees, their teal leaves tinged with gold trim, and all the flowers shine with rainbow auras, fueled by the light of a neon-green sun. As it sinks toward the horizon, it infuses my body with warmth, guiding me toward a lake where diamonds leap off the water in mesmerizing firefly patterns.

"Dylie, quit starin' and start swimmin'!" Elsie shouts out.

She's wearing her rhinestone bathing suit from earlier, and her laughter sparks the air. I race toward the lake, dive into the tropical water.

The water shocks me out of my body, and in an incredible moment of bilocation, I'm playing in the pool with Elysia and Celeste, while my grown-up self sits on a bench watching them, conversing with Jeremiah Bolt.

"I didn't think it was possible to be in two places at once."

Wearing an Empyrea Trucking cap and lightning-streaked swim trunks, Jeremiah Bolt suns himself on a lounge chair. He pulls a cigar out of his mouth, blows blue smoke into the air, forming a small cloud just over the canopy of trees. It starts a small shower over the pool where the kids are swimming, and they shriek, throwing their hands in the air, twirling around and sticking their tongues out to catch raindrops. Then he smiles at me, the gap between his front teeth no longer shaped like a triangle, but an infinity symbol.

"Hey man, you should know by now, everything's possible here. Only your imagination is the limit."

He stares at me intensely, and I follow his eyes to my T-shirt, which proudly proclaims, "THE HEART MEANS EVERYTHING."

"Man, who picks out our wardrobe around here?"

"Here, your clothes are perfect mirrors of your internal state. The fashion industry could learn a thing or two from us."

The wind carries my laughter into the sky, echoing off rocks behind the waterfall. Elysia and Little Celeste are splashing and chasing each other around the lagoon, their giggling effervescing in my chest.

Elysia makes eye contact with me. "Good, Daddy, I'm glad to see you're finally happy."

The word "daddy" rings like a bright bell in my heart. I'm weeping before I can stop myself.

Bolt reaches out, a current of electricity running through us, his cyclone eyes spinning in empathy. "Hey man, ain't nothin' wrong with a few tears. Ain't no law against feeling good either."

Elysia and Celeste gaze at me, like beholding something beautiful. "We love you, Dylie. Always have, always will."

They drift toward a waterfall opening at the far side of the lagoon, and when I see what will happen next, I stand up and yell, "No! Don't go down there! It's too dangerous!"

Bolt grabs my arm. "Relax, man, they're just going to the big lake below."

Both girls and Little Dylan ride the waterfall, squealing "wee!" all the way down. I laugh deeply, my whole body shaking. As Little Dylan, I'm able to share in their fun, my stomach dropping, while they plummet to a second lake below. I just can't believe how connected I feel to everyone—to everything—in this magical place.

"See, I'm not worried about them," Bolt says solemnly. "It's you I'm worried about."

My laughter halts. "Yeah, I know."

"Come on, man. Follow me into the caverns behind the waterfall. I have something important to show you."

∞

I encounter the obsidian darkness yet again, but this time, small torches illuminate the way. Hugging the wall, I trek on the narrow, serpentine trail, taking my time on its dangerous curves.

A subtle aliveness permeates everything, as the chorus from Velvetine's "Safe" echoes throughout the cave, beckoning me home. I sing along with my favorite trance tune, enjoying the resonance of my own voice.

The intervals between torches become shorter, their brightness increasing, the grainy relief of the stone wall growing more visible. I place both hands on its cold surface, a chill running through me. Glittering points in the rocks twinkle like distant stars, somehow aware of my presence.

I come to a clearing made of fine gravel. My heart's pace quickens as I stride toward the light, hearing three distinct voices—soprano, tenor, and bass—singing "Safe" in perfect harmony.

The same gem I saw earlier with Elysia shines in front of me now, its facets broadcasting the song's chords and beats in bursts of white and gold. I have to shield my eyes from its dazzling light.

Oh my God, so that's what music looks like. No wonder I love it so much!

The Advocate, Andalucía, and Jeremiah Bolt have circled around the jewel, their hands joined in seamless connection. They turn to me—beaming—as "Safe" slowly fades out.

"What are you guys doing here? I thought I'd never see all three of you in the same place."

We are the trinity of you. We are one, yet distinct.

In this place, insight is instantaneous. "Oh, okay . . . so you're like the three parts of my personality. I get it now."

We are deeper than your psychology. We are the weavers of your soul's journey; we have composed your experience on Earth.

"Well then, maybe I need new writers. My life hasn't been going all that well, if you haven't noticed."

They break their circle, forming a smaller one around me. Their laughter fills me with love.

But if you look beyond the surface, you will see we've been orchestrating your life ever since you were a little boy. And though there have been roadblocks along the way, they've been necessary to break down your false beliefs, to drive you toward new levels of spiritual knowledge.

"You know, I have sensed an invisible hand guiding me on this journey."

Good. You're learning to live a life of the spirit. It's the ultimate adventure.

"And will you guys always be with me? As weird as it sounds, I've actually gotten used to all of you showing up in my life."

Of course, we are always with you. Together, we constellate the Lover Who Will Never Leave You.

They take my hand, lead me toward the jewel. It's an opal now, rays of color shining through all my cells, illuminating DNA ribbons in their journey through my microscopic universe. I blink, and I'm floating through space, surfing on the rotating arms of galaxies.

"Why can't I just stay here forever?"

You are always here, for paradise is within.

A cathedral of affirmation surges within me, as our circle of four spins faster and faster, like a centrifuge. The spinning ring releases a spire of fire, rocketing me through the ceiling, propelling me to higher and deeper levels of understanding.

"I'll never be alone, right?"

You will be all-one with us. We promise you that.

∞

I rematerialize into the courtroom, empty save for The Advocate, who's dressed in a sea-green robe with gold trim and white sandals. For the first time, I can see some of his perfect, luminous face—it's narrow and angular, cutting through the empty space of the courtroom, his eyes shifting from brown to blue to green, just like Andalucía's. With each change in color, his smile widens.

"Oh my God! I know who you are now."

Indeed. I am He who stands by your side, always defending your essential goodness. I am the Inner Beloved who will never leave you.

An epiphany dawns on me like a lightning bolt. "You and Andalucía are the same being, aren't you?"

The Advocate opens his robe, revealing Andalucía, who stands right by his side. *Together we are the masculine and feminine energies working on your behalf. We appear as separate beings, yet in truth, we are one consciousness.*

"Oh my God, I finally get it now."

They coalesce into a colossal phoenix, exploding in a burst of flames, filling the courtroom with thick smoke.

"Wait, where are you going?" I yell between coughing fits. "Come back!"

We will always be with you, but the time for your resurrection is at hand.

"Don't you mean final judgment?"

They laugh gently. *Isn't it time to dispense with that way of thinking?*

Judge Storm appears in the middle of the smoke like a magician. He embraces me, his only show of compassion during this entire experience. His gaze is unshakable.

"There is no verdict, unless you want there to be. We have given you the tools to be free. You just have to put them into practice."

"But how will I know if I'm on the right path?"

"Just follow the Superhighway of your Soul, and you'll never make a wrong turn."

The tip of Storm's finger glows white hot. He rolls a point at the center of his chest, draws a line up to my head, another down to my heart, and a final line back to him, forming an emerald YIELD sign, its liquid letters rippling. That triangle tips upward, while another one appears and drops downward, both merging into a hexagram. Then he traces a circle around that star as twelve petals unfurl, a lotus blooming from a pool in the middle of his forehead.

He remains silent, smiling enigmatically. Only his eyes shine in the dimming courtroom.

∞

The sun shines down, white clouds rolling through their blue canvas. Red, pink, peach, yellow, and purple roses populate a large garden, waving back and forth in the breeze, while grass blades cut through the wind with their vibrant emerald leaves. In front of a large white gazebo stands a minister in a black robe, patterns on his sash spinning with hurricanes and galaxies. I recognize him immediately.

It's Judge Storm, surrounded by The Advocate and Andalucía. With a wave of their hands, they introduce the wedding party, whose dresses and suits sparkle like gemstone facets. Julie, Marina, and their future husbands are the bridesmaids and groomsmen; Celeste is the matron of honor, Michael my best man. By the time I see Elysia as the flower girl and Luke as the ring bearer, I'm beaming.

In that moment, I know. All is forgiven. When "Jesu, Joy of Man's Desiring" begins to play, my heart accelerates, approaching light speed. Time slows down. It's She, the one I've been waiting for.

Sunlight surrounds her face in a diamond aura. We steeple our hands together as I gaze into her marina eyes.

Finally, I've come home.

Judge Storm announces, "This is the internal marriage—the merging of masculine and feminine energies, the union of all opposites—melted in the divine fire of Love. Dylan, are you ready?"

"Yes. I'm finally ready for my resurrection."

"Good. Then Dylan, do you take Eden to be your wife, forever yours in Holy Matrimony?"

There is no hesitation. "I do."

"And do you, Eden, take Dylan to be your husband, to love him eternally in marriage?"

Tears stream down her face. "Of course I do."

"Then I now pronounce you husband and wife. You may kiss the bride."

We lean in slowly, kiss sensually, as if for the first time. Pressing our foreheads together, we say in unison, "Our love is unconditional—forever changing, yet eternally the same."

Our bodies fuse. Hundreds of petals shower over us, raining on thousands of doves launched into the air. We soon follow suit, soaring into the blue together.

∞

A warm glow suffused my body—my heart soaring—as I walked out of the meditation center into the cold night, zipping up my coat, putting on my stocking cap and gloves. The snow had stopped, but the wind swirled it around the desolate streets like winding snakes, while the fading full moon slid through fingers of rapidly moving clouds. Neon signs in shop windows buzzed, and the occasional car crinkled the flattened snow, but otherwise, the night remained eerily quiet.

After a few minutes, I arrived at a white bridge arched over a small stream, listening to it trickle through the ice. As I stared at the moonlight's reflection in the water, my thoughts turned to Elsie.

I couldn't stop thinking about how she'd hugged me before I left, about how sad her face looked, mirroring my own. She kept saying, "I miss you already, Daddy."

I *did* miss her so much already, and I couldn't wait to see her again. Exhaling slowly, I watched my hot breath smoke out into the darkness.

My hands felt inflamed in my gloves, so I took them off, shoved them in my coat pockets. I had some trouble getting the one glove to go in, and when I pulled it out to feel the object in my bare hand, my heart lurched.

Oh my God. It can't be.

It was the green plastic egg Elsie had given me. I had totally forgotten about it.

I slid the egg out, feeling the ridge where the two halves of plastic met. In the dim light, it appeared grayish.

Thinking some candy would taste especially good right now, I opened it, letting the contents fall squarely into my left palm.

It wasn't the chocolate or jellybeans I was expecting. For a moment, I thought I was still dreaming. Time seemed to stop. There, glinting in the moonlight, was the red ring pop from my dream last night. My breath ballooned, my pulse throbbed in my temples.

Was I hallucinating?

I wondered how Elsie had known about my dream, but there was no way she could have. I'd never told her, and it was too unlikely to be a coincidence. Leaning my head back, I threw my laughter out into the night.

Yes, this trip was a miracle. There was no denying that now.

I stepped tentatively toward the center of the bridge, knowing this jewel was a sign. That warm feeling in my chest intensified, radiating throughout my body, chills lapping the shores of my spine.

Andalucía's voice emanated from that rippling energy: *I am the Eternal Lover who is always with you. Tune into my frequency, for I am the Transmitter of Love.*

Riding right on top of that frequency was Sting's "I'm So Happy I Can't Stop Crying."

I gut-laughed, reveling in this moment of satori[2], knowing exactly who was orchestrating all the music in my life. Yes, Bolt, we are all one in this connected universe. ∧

Jeremiah

---

[2] *Satori* is a Zen term for a sudden moment of awakening, like a lightning bolt. Its effect is usually temporary, but it can be an important stepping stone on the road to enlightenment, or at least on the journey of one's spiritual evolution.

With teary eyes, I stared at the reflected light in the stream. Everything was flowing, my understanding following on the trail of a powerful wake.

I could tell now—I was steeped in the sacred.

Even if I wasn't married to Celeste, and even if we would never be together in the way I wanted, at least in this moment, everything felt right with the world. Besides, with Elsie in the picture, there was plenty to be grateful about. As I looked out into the starry night, a new life beckoned—a life that, God willing—I would somehow find the courage to accept.

TREK III:

A LOVE LIKE IGNITING

— spiritual partners / partnership
— dinner
(↑ = falling) in love / love

caps check

STAGE 1: COUNTDOWN & LIFTOFF

Crossing the Bridge

Are you suffering from a broken heart? *cups?*
Have you given up on Love?
Do you ever wish the longing for _love_ would cease?

(Here's a secret: It doesn't stop, until you embrace—wholeheartedly—*The Greatest Love There Is*.)

Inside you is a bridge whose foundation has been forged in the furnace of your heart. That bridge is the cross of the Dionysian Christ—your unbreakable, untarnishable connection to the divine.

If you allow yourself to fall into silence, you will perceive that subtle inner light, radiating and pulsating endlessly. Welcome to the source of your eternal joy.

Christ said, "You are the light of the world." This is the candle you carry with you in this life—your connection to Spirit. It keeps you alive.

And where there is darkness, that fuse may go out. But you must not refuse it in the traditional sense; no, you must refuse it in the literal sense—spark that fire again!

For it is only an illusion that your light has been snuffed. In truth, it is the inextinguishable flame that will forever fuel your existence.

Your Coronation

So, where shall we start, on this Inner Journey of the heart?

Let's start here. Start now. For in this moment—as in all moments—you are alive. If nothing else, be grateful for that.

Even if your heart is broken. Even if you've been lonely for far too long. Even if those you love have betrayed you. Even if you've lost everything.

In this moment, none of that matters. Just breathe. Naturally, like the ocean tides. For just as the Latin root of the word "spirit" means "breath," so too is breath the root of Spirit. You don't need expensive drugs or fancy techniques to get there. The simple breath will do.

Above all, spirituality should be simple. No need to complicate it with beliefs and dogma. Shut off that ever-flowing tap of the mind.

As you breathe, feel ecstasy bloom within you. This is the presence of the Inner Lover, the One Who Will Never Leave You. She is closer than breath, she is deeper than death, she is the most intimate relationship you will ever have. She puts the "elation" back into relationship by connecting you to the Divine.

She is there for you now, for all time, coronating you as Sovereign of Your Spirit. Watch—bedazzled—as your crown's sparkling jewels shine for eternity.

Your Most Valuable Treasure

Inside you is the Most Valuable Treasure in the Universe—a consciousness, an energy infusing your spirit with aliveness and Love. Think of it as the Divine Diamond, its facets radiating Joy, peace, and your eternal innocence. You always have it available to you.

If you're really attentive, you'll sense that beneath all your human emotions is an ecstasy that can never be diminished. It shines for all time.

This is the Kingdom of God. Keep its paradise close to your heart. Feel it bloom inside you.

Lovers rejoice! For this makes up the essence of who you are—a gem in the Crown of Christ.

Your Tachyon Heart

Within you is *The Greatest Love There Is*, available at all times with its tachyon speed, its infinite comfort. When you truly embrace the essence of Love—what I call the Lover Never Leaving—loneliness becomes a thing of the past. Even if you're alone, you know that at the most fundamental level of reality, you are never alone.

For We Are All One.

When you truly embrace your Inner Lover, you are comfortable being alone, and even better, your connection with others is enhanced. When you truly feel this Ecstatic Electricity surging inside you, you would never need to cheat, because you don't have to go searching for that feeling outside yourself—you already have it. And with the True Love you feel for your partner, you would never want to hurt him or her.

For everything you do honors the both of you.

When all of us truly accept this Lover inside ourselves, we can make realistic commitments and stick with them. We don't promise more than we can deliver. We can honor our commitment because we created it with our partners. It isn't dictated by anyone else.

Not even God.

The nature of this agreement is its commitment to change, its acknowledgement that as couples grow together as individuals, the nature of their agreements change too. In that way, our commitments do not restrict us; on the contrary, they release us. We know that with this person, we've made a commitment to be true to ourselves and each other.

No matter what.

Does this sound too good to be true? Maybe it is. *cut?*

But it's not too God to be true.

Rising into the Tides

We need to recognize Love's true nature. Love asks us to enter the dance as we are—no pretense, no sense getting all worked up over hills and valleys. But we're addicted to that chemical soup we call emotion. We have to realize Love isn't an emotion; it's the power of who we are, and we have to wield it responsibly. Even more so when other people are involved.

You see, Love is the only changing force that works. It brings us joy, yes, but it also brings us great challenges to test the most resilient souls. The question is, are you ready?

If so, dive in. You won't drown. And once you dispense with all this falling in love business, you can then start following Christ's lead and *rise* into Love, instead of always stumbling into and out of it. The sooner you realize that Love is the Crucifixion and Resurrection, the ebb and surge of the tides, the better off we'll all be.

Spiritual Oxygen

We often say that Love is an emotion or power, but in reality, it is a living, breathing organism. It is Life itself.

Even when Love dies in one form, it is reborn in another. Isn't this what Jesus taught, that Love is always resurrecting itself? For Love is constantly in flux—changing from one form to another—in an eternal dance that never ends. That's the beauty and excitement of Life, is it not?

In truth, Love has its own lungs—inhaling joy, exhaling suffering—as we breathe in time with the Cosmic Respiration.

Without that Spiritual Oxygen, our souls would truly asphyxiate.

The Sacred Circuit

When we choose Love, giving and receiving are easy and natural, like breathing. All we have to do is relax into that knowing, like falling into a hammock. Then we can just lie back and enjoy the generous sunshine, the gentle breeze.

In this paradise, you don't really "give" love to yourself or to others; you just connect to the Divine Source and let it shine out on whomever you want. Although you can guide those beams of light, you realize they don't originate with you. They belong to everyone.

This is the Divine Love Cycle illuminated: Connect to the Divine Source, feel its love course through you, let it flow freely to others, and then give it all back to God to complete the Sacred Circuit. As conductor of this Ecstatic Electricity, you'll never lack for love again.

Soul Fuel

As you connect to the Divine Source of Love, breathe it in, feel it surge through you, and let it fill you up until you are overflowing. Because your cup is running over, you offer that excess to others, allowing it to fill them up as well.

Don't worry about running out. Unlike fuel sources on earth, Love is an inexhaustible resource.

While you give this River of Love to others, let it flow back to you. Then give it all back to God so He can extend it to everyone else. Repeat this cycle again the next day.

This is Self-Love, simply stated. There's no indulgence or egotism here. Just fire yourself up, ignite that Soul-Fuel for others. That's all there is to it.

For you are a star. Share your brilliant Incandescence with all you meet.

STAGE 2: BREAKING FREE
OF EARTH'S GRAVITY

Redeeming the Eden Within

L ove should be simple and straightforward—but oh, dear Lord!—how we love to convolute it with drama. We don't understand that residing within romantic love *is* heartbreak—coiled up and ready to strike—like that serpent who first tempted us in Eden. And just like gravity, what goes up must come down. We can't escape this physical and spiritual law.

The truth is, we love the emotional rollercoaster romance brings—all its dizzying highs and depressing lows. Of course we crave the intensity and passion of the beginning, with all its promises of Forever Love; but believe it or not, we are just as addicted to the breakup, when we come crashing back down to Earth. Here, we become justified in our resentment toward the former beloved, or even Love itself. We also thrill to tell our tales of being crucified by our ex, or how deliciously we crucified him or her.

Seriously folks, we need to get a new hobby. It's just not working for us. We need to reinvent romance, perhaps tear it down to its foundation. We have to return to the Garden *before* the Fall by redeeming the Eden Within—our essential, innocent nature.

So how can we learn to love each other, especially as life partners, without all this unnecessary drama? It starts with opening up to our vulnerability, owning our sun and shadow sides, and communicating honestly. These are simple steps we complicate needlessly.

To the Soul, loving is easy, like breathing. But to the Ego[3]? I think I hear it about to hyperventilate.

---

[3] For the purposes of this book, I define Ego as the antithesis of the Soul or Love, which is our true nature. However, the Ego should not be thought of as an enemy to destroy or to eliminate, but rather more benignly, as a fertilizer. From its creative synthesis in the soil of our souls blooms the beautiful flowers of our awakened selves, the blissful return to our spiritual home as Divine Beings—the ultimate goal of our evolution as a species.

Writing a New Script

Caps

When it comes to romantic love, we know the script by heart, don't we? We meet an attractive person, date and wine and dine, fall madly in love, have lots of hot sex, get engaged and plan for the wedding, get married, have kids, buy a nice big house, accumulate a lot of stuff, and then live happily ever after.

(Or is it die unhappily ever after? Who came up with this scenario, anyway? I think we need new writers.)

I wonder, are we following romance's directives, or did we invent this script, and then play it—and replay it ad nauseam, ad infinitum—in romantic movies, books, and songs? Either way, I don't think the source of the influence matters. It's institutional heart-washing, no matter what.

caps

The truth is, we have the right to write our own love scripts as free Children of God. It's more fun that way. We get enough rules in life as it is.

Love is supposed to be a Gift of Infinite Surprise, not a recycled Christmas gift. We have no idea of Love's true nature. To limit it to mere romance and sentiment seems akin to blasphemy.

Love can't be reduced to cards and candy, flowers and candlelight dinners, great sex and amazing dates. No, Love is far greater than that. To accept a deeper, more mature love, we have to switch our focus from the body—and even from the mind—to the Spirit. Soul first.

The only way Love can flourish is if it grows roots in the Spirit, if it blooms from the Heart. Anything else is a mere shadow of the luminous love experience. *caps*

The Only Game in Town

We tend to look for Love the same way we look for a job—trying to match our qualifications with our potential partner's qualifications, marking off our checklist of "Desirable Qualities for Our Perfect Partner," and entering into those early dates like job interviews, both as interviewee and interviewer. As interviewee, we put our best foot forward, trying to impress this person; as interviewer, we ask our list of questions to see if this person would be a good fit for Me, Inc.

Can we dispense with this please?

Love asks that we don't put on airs to be bigger and better than we are, for she knows how easily the ego balloon can pop. All Love asks is we come as we are, leaving all pretense at the door. She wants us to breathe comfortably inside her tropical hammock.

But unfortunately, Ego suffers from constrictive thinking; it believes Love is a game. There are winners and losers, and someone has to keep score. It cries, "But love is pain! Love is torture! We must sacrifice ourselves on its demanding altar!"

Do you see how ridiculous this is? How funny?

Unfortunately, the Ego isn't laughing. It rarely laughs, unless it's at someone else's expense.

Yet Love knows she's the only game in town. If you want to get caught up in competition and scorecards, that's fine. You have that freedom. But Love knows the game is only there for your infinite expansion—and yes, dear Ego—even for your eternal enjoyment.

The Eden Within Need

Possessive love is the Ego's game, where Love is exclusive—never inclusive—and is about meeting our own needs instead of seeing that in Love, there are no needs. In Spirit we set our partners free by giving them permission to be who they are. That's the ultimate *caps?* freedom.

Ego would have us believe our beloved *is* God, but that's a clever sidestep. *Love* is God. We bow down before Divinity, not each other. In this way, we don't serve each other's needs, which Love fulfills effortlessly, but rather our highest call as humans—our Ultimate Completion in God. Although our partners can't complete us, Love can, because that is who we are at our core.

Love is an inexhaustible fountain constantly quenching our thirst. It offers us an oasis in this desert called Life.

from procreation to cocreation

Slipping into Our Spiritual Skin

→ Time for a New Paradigm

If we're serious about equality in our relationships, then we have to relinquish this paradigm of submission and dominance, the *code* of the animal kingdom. While *this* works well for animals and may have worked well for us at one point, it no longer serves us. We have to evolve beyond it. If one partner is submissive and the other dominant, there can be no equality, by definition. The power dynamic is lopsided.

We also have to ditch the part of the romantic paradigm founded on hormones and endorphins. When we fall in love, we're selecting a mate based on genetic desirability, and the high is designed to last as long as we couple and have children. Romance's wonder and magic soon wear off after that. But if we're serious about spiritual love, we have to seek mates not on the basis of *pro*-creation, but *co*-creation. In the latter, the children we birth can be actual human beings, but our offspring can also become the new selves we create as a result of our spiritual partnership. We can grow via mitosis or metamorphosis, or a creative interplay of both. It's up to us.

This is where choice comes in. The only way our species will survive is if we evolve from "survival of the fittest" to "spiritual of the lightest." In that way, Christ can come again into our hearts for the Second Coming, an event that ignites from the inside out.

In that ecstatic moment, transformation becomes like breathing. We can molt out of this animal skin and *slip* into our spiritual skin, where eternity resonates in our cells, beckoning us home.

Love Is Its Own Evolution

Many of us have been taught that when we feel an intense connection with someone, it should be romantic, and eventually (or immediately) sexual. We're also taught that romantic love is the end game, the ultimate goal.

But it's not. It's only the beginning.

Romance is the first blush of springtime, an adolescent love. It's not meant to last, because we'd never grow; we'd be blissed out all the time. We have to realize there is more than one progression to Love.

Within the energy of Love is its own evolution. We don't have to follow some prescribed plan, whether it's from our culture, our family, or our own need to control. Within that first meeting is the DNA of that love, from birth to death. In other words, Love is its own organism. We'd be smart to follow its directives.

Ultimately, we need to let heart connections be what they are naturally. Not graft some romantic fantasy onto it. Not inject some sexual chemistry into it.

For what is romance, but a costume we dress around Love's Great Light?

A More Perfect Union

Many will label the romantic phase as an illusion or fantasy, but this judgment is too harsh. The process of falling in love is perfect because it's foolproof—it almost always achieves its aims. Nature's goal in the mating process is to produce offspring of a varied genetic pool through serial monogamy. No one has to think about this process; it's instinctual.

Sooner or later, the process is complete, and the romantic phase ends, yet most of us want it to continue because it's so blissful. We hang onto it for dear life, blindly hoping it will continue. But it won't. Once it has found completion—another word for perfection—then it has taken its last breath. This is an organic process that cannot be artificially extended.

If we desire the Great Love we've always dreamed about, we have to stop letting instinct be the driver of our behavior. In order to go from unconscious to conscious, we have to let intention rule us, not instinct. We have to move from the primal to the spiritual paradigm, from procreation to co-creation. It's the only way our love will survive.

The offspring of spiritual partnerships can then be psychological healing and spiritual wholeness, consummated by our connection with the Divine. We can then redeem Eden as each of us returns to the perfected state of the Primordial Couple.

We will then shepherd each other back into *The Greatest Romance There Is*—the return to Union in God.

Call for a Greater Love

Can we move beyond this mammalian love? Can we extend our sphere of love beyond our mates, our offspring, our family and friends?

And most of all, can we move into a love that includes all, excludes none?

We have to. If we don't, we'll end up distrusting, fearing—and worst of all—despising everyone outside our personal sphere.

Our special relationships can be impediments to Greater Love, to the next step of evolution of our species. We have to move from local to Universal Love, from conditional to Unconditional Love.

Our survival as a species depends on it.

STAGE 3: ENTERING SYNCHRONOUS ORBIT

God's Greatest Gift

Caps

Relationship is one of God's greatest gifts. It is how the Fundamental Unity of Creation experiences itself via the Vehicle of Separation. Separation may indeed be an illusion, as the spiritual adepts say, but it's a necessary illusion, for it serves a crucial purpose—as a teaching tool to see our level of distance from God in each other's eyes.

Christ said, "For wherever two or three gather in my name, there I am with them." This is a profound truth. We are usually not aware of that divine connection in isolation, even if we look in a mirror. No, the most effective mirror is in the eyes of another, who can reflect back to us our own interplay of light and dark.

This Mirror of Love and Truth is not just for romantic relationships—it's for any relationship where a deep connection and serious commitment to spiritual growth exists. You love the other as much as you love yourself, because the ultimate spiritual truth is this: In the One there are Many, and in the Many, there is One.

The Holographic Nature of Love

The kind of love I'm talking about is not selfish, does not indulge the Ego or exalt one person over another. No, in a relationship of equals, that just won't do. For the love I'm talking about connects us to that Divine Source, where we merely see ourselves as one part of Creation, as one person among many who deserves acknowledgement as a sacred being.

The beauty of spiritual relationships is they aren't confined to romantic love. Since we're all connected as one in the spiritual realm, we can forge deep, long-lasting connections with any of our brothers and sisters on Earth. It's like a hologram: The imprint of the whole can be found in each of its parts, so each of us is a representation of the One who is Many, the Many who are One.

Though we can take this journey alone, there's no need to. We have our fellow Suns of God to help us along the way, as we move from fragmentation and brokenness to integration and wholeness. All it takes is courage, and willingness to explore the limitless God-Within.

Our True Happily-Ever-After

In the mirror of your partner's face, can you see the snarl behind the smile? The untamed wildness within? If so, you're starting to get the picture.

No doubt when you fell in love, you clearly saw the other's light. But now it's time to see the darkness as well.

(Both are projections, by the way. The Light and Dark dance within you too.)

In the blackest fungal depths, romance is meant to be crucified, and to die. We think that's the end, but it's only a transition to a greater state. We must have the courage to walk through "the valley of the shadow of death" as a couple, perhaps with some divine assistance. Once we come out the other side, we can be resurrected into a higher form of Love. Then Eden can be redeemed, and we can return to Paradise, fully awakened.

Only then can we have our True Happily-Ever-After.

Our Birthright of Light

L ove connects us to our Higher Self—the one that lives in the light all the time, the one that only sees the good in others. People think the falling-in-love stage is an illusion or a fantasy, where our blinders come on and we refuse to see the negative traits of the other. And perhaps there is some truth to this. But in Love, we enter the mystical, heavenly state that is our birthright; we rise up to meet our destiny in the Light of Love.

That light is the Lantern of God. We should cherish its presence, like a dear lover. hide

Yet how we ~~fear sharing~~ our little light, for fear of being ridiculed or condemned. How strange this fear is.

For our Light is all we truly have to give.

The Divine Photographer

When we experience heartbreak, there's a difference between being broken apart and broken open. When we're broken apart, we fall to pieces, like shattered glass. We gave our heart completely to someone, and now that he or she isn't giving it back, we're devastated. It's hard to recover from a Total Wreckage of the Heart.

On the other hand, when we allow our hearts to be broken open instead, there's hope within the hurt. The wound doesn't cut quite as deep; we can heal. Being broken open is like splitting a pistachio—the hard shell is gone and only the nutmeat remains, green and vulnerable to the air. You may feel exposed, but it's better than being one of those sealed-shut nuts, that no matter what you do—short of using a hammer—you'll never get the damn thing open.

So now there is a fissure where the Light of Love can break through, shining through our darkest days. In that space, instead of experiencing the shattering and eventual shuttering of our soul's cracked windows, we can feel our heart's aperture opening wide to receive the Ecstatic Christ—the Divine Photographer and Camera all rolled into one—who will develop us into a luminous ~~work of art.~~ *cups?* *masterpiece*

The Physics of Love

caps ?

Falling in love ignites a nuclear reaction in our hearts. Though the energy it releases is powerful, it's ultimately neutral. It's up to us what we do with it.

caps ? At first, romance catalyzes a fusion reaction. We melt and merge with our Beloved, and in that process, an incredible amount of energy is released, drawing on the star-fuel that created the elements for our bodies. In that high-energy state, we feel we can radiate as binary stars forever. *with our partners*

But as fusion breaks down, we are forced to rely more on fission. After our atomic bond splits apart, an incredible explosion occurs, threatening to unleash emotional devastation, unless we can harness that energy for Divine Love. That is why we call this phase Falling Out of Love, because there is a nuclear fallout emitting deadly radiation. Many of our couplings are poisoned as a result.

We can also think about romantic coupling in terms of annihilation, when two opposing particles collide and destroy each other, releasing even more energy than fusion. But in the best-case scenario of Love, we do not destroy ourselves. Only the Ego is annihilated, and that explosion launches our souls into inner space.

You see, Despite what some "spiritual" types may tell you, Ego isn't all bad; it does have a purpose. But once it has served its purpose—for holding up the Illusion of Separation—its explosion—or implosion, depending on your perspective—is quite spectacular. Then you can jettison those no-longer-needed booster rockets.

Just be careful, though. For when a star goes supernova, it takes out the whole blasted neighborhood. But when it ejects its stellar matter into space like dandelion seeds, it fertilizes space for new stars.

You see, Ego is just compost. It makes the soil fertile for Soul to bloom.

But in its destruction is enfolded a new Creation.

Love Transformed

Even if we've been in love before, we come to its invitation totally ill-prepared. We can say that we're going to be more reasonable, that we're going to take it slower, but when we meet face to face with the Beautiful Beloved, all bets are off.

As fun as the romance rollercoaster is, it's an unconscious process. Nature has made it nearly foolproof: Anyone can fall in love. But it takes wisdom and courage to stay there.

If we want our couplings to last—or at least be more fulfilling—we have to become more conscious in our relationships. We have to learn how to manage this incredible nuclear energy released when we fall in love. We have to take it slow: friends first, lovers second—and if we get there—spiritual partners last.

This is the spiritual path of relationship, focused on growth and working toward Unconditional Love. It's not about security, or even happiness anymore. It's about wholeness. It's a form of yoga, with God-Union as the ultimate goal. No longer will your partner be a screen to project all your fears onto; now your partner will be a mirror to see yourself, a window to view your luminous future as a realized Son or Daughter of God.

Just imagine if we entered into relationship not because of lust or emotional need, but because of our spiritual desire to better ourselves and our partners, to improve our lives with the richness of Divine Love.

My God. Then our relationships could be truly transformed.

A New Adventure

What I'm proposing is driving into our relationships with our Soul's high beams on, not riding blindly in the dark. We want to arrive at our destination in peace, not in pieces.

Don't worry, we can still enjoy the romance phase and intense connection, but we must not go out of our minds. We can surrender to Love and still remain awake. That's the challenge. *Caps?*

The first blush of romance is an initiation, an invitation to Love's Dance, where we can eventually choreograph all the unhealed parts of ourselves into a beautiful routine.

Ultimately, you have to know what brought you and your partner together in the first place, and why you have such a strong connection. Chances are you both share some issue to be resolved, some wound to be healed. You're together until you become whole in Love. Of course you can stay together as long as you like, but once you've dismantled your heart's roadblocks with that person, the purpose for your connection has been fulfilled. *caps? caps?*

And if you fall in love again with the same partner, a New Adventure can begin! For you see, there are no rules here. You make it up as you go, letting Love lead the way.

STAGE 4: REENTRY INTO PARADISE

Love's Expansion

W e've all suffered heartbreak—even betrayal—in romantic love. It seems woven into the experience. Yet in order to break out of it, we have to change ourselves and our preconceptions about Love.

So I propose what Gary Zukav calls a spiritual partnership: "a relationship between equals for the purpose of spiritual growth." And that growth is the key. It's the only way our Happily-Ever-After Fairy-Tale will come true, in any real sense. We have to realize the Love we feel with our partners is a natural manifestation of Christ—the Lover Who Will Never Leave Us. We have to cultivate a relationship with our Inner Lover, the only one who can truly show us Unconditional Love. Only then can we work on achieving that kind of love with another person.

And once you truly connect with that Christ energy, your relationships will be revolutionized, for Love never stops growing—it expands exponentially, coloring the palette of infinity. Indeed, that is its nature. For the expansion of Love and the Universe is the same thing.

215

Spiritual Intercourse: Couples as God Force

Once we've worked through our power struggles as couples and set them aside, we can then move on to the next phase of Love—the Resurrection, where the River of the Risen flows unimpeded. We can then focus on the soul work we came to Earth to do.

In order to move beyond the body-mind, we have to dive deeper into our Soul connection. After lovemaking—which relaxes the body and is Spiritual foreplay for the soul—the couple can let their bodies sleep while their minds remain alert. Through this Soul-Trekking, they can explore the Universe as their Eternal Playground. In this space, they actually become one since their astral bodies—as finer filaments of energy—can merge in ways their physical bodies cannot.

This is Spiritual Intercourse, where couples revel in their Ecstatic Union, performing instantaneous soul scans to experience complete communication. In this blessed blissful state, souls can then read the imprint of the other and absorb their partner's energy patterns into themselves, fusing their best qualities together to strengthen their atomic bond. Nothing is hidden and souls can heal their psychological wounds through this Ecstatic Energy Exchange, as another type of God communion.

Now as a Unified Soul Force, couples can surge ahead, charged as electrified conduits for God's work on this planet.

And beyond.

The Eternal Playground

Caps !

With our <u>soul</u> companions on Earth, we are of course free to explore all the beauty and adventures our Mother Planet has to offer during the day. But at night, when we are naked in Spirit—stripped of skin and myelin—now intimate in body and soul—we will achieve complete liberation.

In this emancipated state, our lovemaking will not be about orgasm; rather, in our vulnerability, we will open up new chasms to leap into, where we will voyage into the equally wondrous universes of Inner Space. Soaring through these subatomic skies, we will burst through horizon after horizon, knowing and respecting no boundaries. *Caps !*

After integrating this Micro/Cosmos into ourselves, life is then transformed into an Eternal Playground, where our reclaimed innocence leads the way. This is what Christ meant when he said you must enter the Kingdom of God as little children. You thought your partner held the keys to that kingdom, but now, when you look down at your hand, you realize you were holding them all along.

But it was fun to play the game anyway. A little cosmic hide and seek, cops and robbers, just to delight in the Joy of Creation.

Tuning to the Divine Orchestra

The best lovers know that intercourse does not just describe the sexual act. They know it is more profoundly a way of being, in which there is some type of intercourse flowing between them in every moment, whether it's having a soulful conversation, sharing an enjoyable activity, or just spending time together in silence. Sex closes that circuit on the physical plane as the Alpha and Omega of our Christ Connection. In this state, no foreplay or afterglow exists, because all converges into the Radiant Present, where sex is simply a free energetic exchange between two individuals.

If that depth of intimacy seems hard to achieve, it's not. You opened up to it intuitively when you fell in love, when you were constantly aware of your connection with your partner. All you have to do is bring that awareness back to yourself and your lover, like a reset button.

Remember, true intimacy is spiritual, not physical, for the body is only a conduit for the Ecstatic Electricity of God. With your soul properly tuned, you will hear the Divine Orchestra playing infinitely for your amusement.

Spiritual Foreplay

Sex is Spiritual Foreplay because of the tremendous energy released during intercourse. That energy pools and rises in the second chakra, and when it's released during climax into the northern chakras, the portals to creation are opened. We can then walk through them, if we're willing. In this way, sexual energy can be harnessed and cultivated, not suppressed or moralized.

caps? But the storm of sex isn't necessary to reach these portals. Instead of relying on sex to enter that still, silent state of the Divine, we can use various metaphysical tools like prayer or meditation to access that state at will. Then we don't even need sex, at least not psychologically.

I know, I know, we miss out on all that pleasure and fun. But here's the secret: Genitals aren't needed to feel that Ecstatic Electricity. Only God is.

Gateway to God

When we fall in love with others, their Divinity and Radiance are revealed, their spirits unsheathed. They become the Gateway to God.

The problem is, we soon mistake that gateway for the Source, which is God, not our partner. This is why we put our lovers on pedestals. If we believe they are the Source of Love, why wouldn't we glorify them?

Yes, they are Divine Beings connected to God, but we must not mistake them for the Source. Our fall from Paradise is then inevitable.

Although your partner is there to help you see your own Divinity, neither of you is God. But the Love between you is.

The Pedestal Inside You

In most romantic couplings, we put a lot of pressure on our partners to meet all our needs, as if they're the answer to all our prayers. And the truth is, most of us deflate or explode from all this pressure. It may be one of the fundamental problems in relationships.

One person is not a smorgasbord where all your appetites can be sated. Certainly, you can be emotionally and sexually faithful to one person, but you can't expect them to be everything to you. That's God's job, not theirs.

Get them off the pedestals, folks. But gently. We don't want anyone getting hurt. You have to realize the pedestal is inside you. And when you climb it, it leads to a stairway shining up toward the Radiance of Spirit, where the Rainbow Symphony of Souls explodes with applause.

The Ultimate You

For all you lonely and heartbroken souls out there, consider this: What if **<u>YOU</u>** are the person you've been waiting for?

Like me, I know you've spent a lot of time looking for the "right" person. Well, look no further—that right person is you! You're the one who has to live with yourself anyway.

While a relationship can be a faster way to grow spiritually, it isn't required. You can step into the Ultimate You, all by yourself. You just have to commit to this process of soul expansion. *Caps* ?

And once you've stepped into your full potential as an Enlightened Sun of God, just think of the partner you will attract! He or she will be one luminous mirror, that's for sure.

But don't initiate your own growth process just for the promise of the right partner. You may never meet that person. You may set up such high expectations that no one can realistically meet. And most importantly, you'd be doing it for the wrong reasons. If you grow for yourself, you'll be able to grow with others; if you evolve just for that other person, you may never meet the Ultimate You.

The real romance is your Dance with the Divine anyway. That love affair is eternal and perfect—it will never let you down.

And once you surrender to that loving energy, God is there, joyfully racing to embrace you.

Encore: You Are a Song of God

The Benevolent Tsunami is speeding your way. The question is, are you ready?

Since this storm is an internal event, there's no need for alarm. You are safe.

I know you fear the storm's power, but it *can* be harnessed for good. Riding the Zeitgeist Lightning was never for the faint of heart.

You want to wait for the right timing? My friend, the timing is *now*, for the tsunami's companion, the Hurricane, is winding the clock faster. Haven't you noticed time speeding up?

Tick-tock, tick-tock. Your heart is beating—accelerating—knocking on the door of your sternum. Go ahead and add the melody, the harmony, if you really want to show off. But come as you are. No pretense please.

Yes, it's crunch time: Are you ready to unleash the Music of Love? Are you ready to be a Song of God?

I pray that you are. For the Divine Orchestra is tuning to your readiness.

LALNL SOUNDTRACK
(in order of appearance)

1. "Losing My Religion" by R.E.M.
2. "Run to the Water" by Live
3. "A Kiss to Build a Dream On" by Louis Armstrong
4. "The World I Know" by Collective Soul
5. "Gone" by David Holmes
6. "Hemorrhage (in My Hands)" by Fuel
7. "Just Like Heaven" by The Cure
8. "Zombie" by The Cranberries
9. *In Search of Sunrise 3*, mix album by DJ Tiësto
10. "Nothing Compares 2 U" by Sinéad O'Connor
11. "Tears from the Moon (Tiësto In Search of Sunrise Remix)" by Conjure One, featuring Sinéad O'Connor
12. "I Have Put Out the Light" by James Holden
13. *The K & D Sessions*, mix album by Kruder and Dorfmeister
14. "Shivers" by Armin van Buuren
15. "Everytime We Touch" by Cascada
16. "We Are Alive" by Paul Van Dyk
17. "Ghost Town" by Adam Lambert
18. "Principles of Lust" by Enigma
19. "I Still Haven't Found What I'm Looking For" by U2
20. "Comfortably Numb" by Pink Floyd
21. "Waiting for the Worms" by Pink Floyd
22. "So Caught Up (Original Mix)" by Max Graham, featuring Neev Kennedy

23. "White Wedding" by Billy Idol
24. "Inside" by Sting
25. "This Year's Love" by David Gray
26. *The Mask and Mirror*, album by Loreena McKennitt
27. "With or Without You" by U2
28. "Eternal Flame" by The Bangles
29. "Sacred Love" by Sting
30. "Fragile" by Sting
31. "Let Go" by Frou Frou
32. "The Dolphin's Cry" by Live
33. "Rainy Day Women #12 & 35" by Bob Dylan
34. "Walk Like an Egyptian" by The Bangles
35. "Higher Love" by Steve Winwood
36. "Stereo Hearts" by Gym Class Heroes, featuring Adam Levine
37. *Moonlight Sonata*, Piano Sonata No. 14 in C# minor, by Ludwig van Beethoven
38. *Adagio for Strings* by Samuel Barber
39. "Amazing Grace" as performed by Celtic Woman
40. "Two Tickets to Paradise" by Eddie Money
41. "Ode to Joy," 4th movement of Symphony No. 9 in D minor, by Ludwig van Beethoven
42. "Vertigo" by U2
43. "Adventure of a Lifetime" by Coldplay
44. "Safe (Wherever You Are) [Rank 1 Remix—AVB Intro Edit]" by Velvetine
45. "Jesu, Joy of Man's Desiring," chorale from *Heart and Mouth and Deed and Life*, Cantata no. 147, by Johann Sebastian Bach
46. "I'm So Happy I Can't Stop Crying" by Sting

RECOMMENDED READING

Adamson, Sophie. *Through the Gateway of the Heart: Accounts and Experiences with MDMA and Other Empathogenic Substances*, 2nd ed., Solarium Press, 1985.

Anonymous. *Christ in You*. DeVorss Publications, 2010.

Bach, Richard. *One*. Dell Publishing, 1988.

Bonheim, Jalaja. *The Hunger for Ecstasy: Fulfilling the Soul's Need for Passion and Intimacy*. Daybreak Books, 2001.

Cameron, Julia. *The Artist's Way: A Spiritual Path to Higher Creativity*. Tarcher/Putnam, 1992.

Coehlo, Paulo. *The Alchemist*. Harper One, 1993.

Cohen, Alan. *Rising in Love: The Journey into Light*. Eden Company, 1983.

Curtis, Brent, and John Eldredge. *The Sacred Romance: Drawing Closer to the Heart of God*. Thomas Nelson, 1997.

Dass, Ram. *Be Here Now*. Harmony Books, 1978.

——. *Be Love Now: The Path of the Heart*. Harper One, 2010.

Eadie, Betty J. *Embraced by the Light*. Gold Leaf Press, 1992.

Edwards, Gene. *The Divine Romance*. Tyndale House, 1984.

Ferrini, Paul. *Creating a Spiritual Partnership: A Guide to Growth and Happiness for Couples on the Path*. Heartways Press, 1998.

——. *Dancing with the Beloved*. Heartways Press, 2001.

——. *The Gospel According to Jesus: A New Testament for Our Time*. Heartways Press, 2009.

——. *The Hidden Jewel: Discovering the Radiant Light Within*. Heartways Press, 2007.

——. *I Am the Door: Exploring the Christ Presence Within*. Heartways Press, 1999.

——. *The Laws of Love: A Course in Spiritual Mastery Part 1.* Heartways Press, 2004.

——. *The Power of Love: A Course in Spiritual Mastery Part 2.* Heartways Press, 2004.

——. *The Presence of Love: A Course in Spiritual Mastery Part 3.* Heartways Press, 2006.

——. *When Love Comes as a Gift: Meeting the Soul Mate in This Life.* Heartways Press, 2010.

——. *The Wisdom of Self: Authentic Experience and the Journey to Wholeness.* Heartways Press, 1992.

——. *The Wounded Child's Journey into Love's Embrace.* Heartways Press, 1991.

Fox, Matthew. *The Coming of the Cosmic Christ: The Healing of Mother Earth and the Birth of the Global Renaissance.* Harper & Row, 1988.

Goldsmith, Joel. *The Infinite Way.* DeVorss Publications, 1956.

Hawkins, David R. *Discovery of the Presence of God: Devotional Nonduality.* Veritas Publishing, 2007.

——. *The Eye of the I: From Which Nothing Is Hidden.* Veritas Publishing, 2001.

——. *I: Reality and Subjectivity.* Veritas Publishing, 2003.

——. *Letting Go: The Pathway of Surrender.* Veritas Publishing, 2012.

——. *Transcending the Levels of Consciousness: The Stairway to Enlightenment.* Veritas Publishing, 2006.

Hesse, Hermann. *Siddhartha: An Indian Tale.* Penguin, 1999.

Hubbard, Barbara Marx. *The Revelation: Our Crisis Is a Birth.* Nataraj Publishing, 1993.

Jampolsky, Gerald. *Love Is Letting Go of Fear.* Celestial Arts, 2004.

Johnson, Robert A. *Ecstasy: Understanding the Psychology of Joy.* Harper Collins, 1987.

—. *Owning Your Own Shadow: Understanding the Dark Side of the Psyche.* Harper Collins, 1991.

—. *WE: Understanding the Psychology of Romantic Love.* Harper & Row, 1983.

Levine, Stephen and Ondrea. *Embracing the Beloved: Relationship as a Path of Awakening.* Anchor Books, 1995.

Martel, Yann. *Life of Pi: A Novel.* Harcourt, 2001.

Moore, Thomas. *Soul Mates: Honoring the Mysteries of Love and Relationship.* Harper Collins, 1994.

—. *The Soul of Sex: Cultivating Life as an Act of Love.* Harper Collins, 1998.

O'Brien, Tim. *The Things They Carried.* Mariner Books, 2009.

O'Donohue, John. *Anam Cara: A Book of Celtic Wisdom.* Harper Collins, 1997.

Paulsen, Norman. *Christ Consciousness: Emergence of the Pure Self Within.* Solar Logos Foundation, 2002.

Peterson, Eugene H. *The Message: The Bible in Contemporary Language.* NavPress, 2018.

Redfield, James. *The Celestine Prophecy: An Adventure.* Warner Books, 1993.

Rohr, Richard. *The Universal Christ: How a Forgotten Reality Can Change Everything We See, Hope For, and Believe.* Convergent Books, 2019.

Schucman, Helen. *A Course in Miracles.* The Foundation for Inner Peace, 1992.

Tolle, Eckhart. *The Power of Now: A Guide to Spiritual Enlightenment.* Namaste Publishing, 2004.

Vaughan-Lee, Llewellyn. *The Bond with the Beloved: The Mystical Relationship of the Lover and the Beloved.* The Golden Sufi Center, 1993.

Walsch, Neale Donald. *Communion with God.* Berkley Publishing Group, 2000.

——. *The Complete Conversations with God.* Putnam & Hampton Roads Publishing, 2005.

——. *Friendship with God: An Uncommon Dialogue.* Berkley Publishing Group, 1999.

——. *Home with God: In a Life That Never Ends.* Atria Books, 2007.

Weiss, Brian. *Only Love Is Real: A Story of Soulmates Reunited.* Warner Books, 1996.

Williamson, Marianne. *A Return to Love: Reflections on the Principles of A Course in Miracles.* Harper Perennial, 1992.

Yogananda, Paramahansa. *The Divine Romance: Collected Talks and Essays on Realizing God in Daily Life Vol. II.* Self-Realization Fellowship, 1986.

——. *Journey to Self-Realization: Collected Talks and Essays on Realizing God in Daily Life Vol. III.* Self-Realization Fellowship, 1997.

——. *Man's Eternal Quest: Collected Talks and Essays on Realizing God in Daily Life Vol. I.* Self-Realization Fellowship, 1982.

——. *The Second Coming of Christ: The Resurrection of the Christ Within You.* Self-Realization Fellowship, 2004.

Young, Sarah. *Jesus Calling: Enjoying Peace in His Presence.* Thomas Nelson, 2004.

Young, William P. *The Shack: Where Tragedy Confronts Eternity.* Windblown Media, 2007.

Zukav, Gary. *The Seat of the Soul: 25th Anniversary Edition with a Study Guide.* Simon & Schuster, 2014.

——. *Spiritual Partnership: The Journey to Authentic Power.* Harper One, 2010.

Zweig, Connie and Steve Wolf. *Romancing the Shadow: Illuminating the Dark Side of the Soul.* Ballantine Books, 1997.

GRATITUDES

A book is always the product of many minds, hands, and hours, so I'd like to offer my heartfelt gratitude to the following individuals:

Gratitude #1: Flagstaff artist Jason Oberman painted the beautiful artwork that appears on the cover of this book. It is a visually arresting image that fits my vision of *Like a Lover Never Leaving* perfectly. People often say not to judge a book by its cover, but I couldn't ask for more than to be judged on the artistic merit of his work.

Gratitude #2: The following writing professionals provided invaluable guidance, encouragement, and editorial insight: The Coconino Community College (CCC) Writer's Group; Jerry Baker and Sandra Dihlmann, English instructors at CCC; Patricia Nelson, agent for Marsal Lyon Literary Agency; Cherri Randall, Assistant Professor of English at the University of Pittsburgh at Johnstown; and Craig Grossman at Cawing Crow Press. Their expertise helped make *Like a Lover Never Leaving* the best book it could be.

Gratitude #3: The books of these spiritual teachers have been trusted companions on this amazing Soul Trek: Deepak Chopra, Wayne Dyer, Betty Eadie, Joel Goldsmith, David R. Hawkins, Barbara Marx Hubbard, Valerie Hunt, Sue Monk Kidd, Shirley MacLaine, Anita Moorjani, Carolyn Myss, and Neale Donald Walsch mirrored back to me my true spiritual essence; Leo Buscaglia, Alan Cohen, Gene Edwards, and Gerald Jampolsky reminded me of the beauty, simplicity, and power of Love; Brendon Burchard, Julia Cameron, Paulo Coehlo, Hermann Hesse, Yann Martel, Tim

O'Brien, and William P. Young inspired me with their creative works; Amit Goswami, Brian Greene, Michio Kaku, Lynne McTaggart, Gary Renard, Carl Sagan, Michael Talbot, and Fred Alan Wolf reignited my passion for this strange yet wonderful Universe we live in; Joseph Campbell, Aldous Huxley, Stanislav Grof, Robert A. Johnson, and Robert Monroe sent me on voyages deep into the heart of my spirit; Carlos Castaneda, Dan Millman, Mark Nepo, Parker Palmer, Eckhart Tolle, and Marianne Williamson pointed the way to the wisdom of my own Inner Teacher; Ram Dass, Matthew Fox, Paul Ferrini, Norman Paulsen, Helen Schucman, Paramahansa Yogananda, and Sarah Young illuminated the path to the Cosmic Christ within; Richard Bach, Jalaja Bonheim, Stephen and Ondrea Levine, Thomas Moore, John O'Donohue, Brian Weiss, Steve Wolf, Gary Zukav, and Connie Zweig reaffirmed the powerful potential—and undeniable reality—of soulmates and spiritual partners; and James Redfield's *Celestine Prophecy* catalyzed this incredible spiritual journey two decades ago. Dear God, what a ride!

Gratitude #4: My wife and soulmate, Megan, was generous enough to give me honest and helpful critiques, and even more impressively, to put up with the countless hours I spent working on this project. She probably thought my work on it would never end. Sometimes, I wondered too.

Gratitude #5: My Ultimate Soulmate, Jesus Christ—Lord, Lover, and Light of our souls—lifted me up to write this book in his divine embrace. Without his initial inspiration and quiet guidance, this book would not exist, and I never would have returned to writing in the first place. It is his benevolent spirit that pulses in the open spaces of these pages.

ABOUT THE AUTHOR

Jeremy A. Martin was born in Hershey, Pennsylvania (Chocolatetown, U.S.A.) and lived in nearby Palmyra until he was eighteen. After graduating from Palmyra High School, he moved to Galesburg, Illinois, to attend Knox College for his Bachelor of Arts in English, then continued his studies at Eastern Washington University in Spokane, Washington, to receive his Master of Fine Arts in Creative Writing. In addition, he has served in Literacy AmeriCorps Pittsburgh, worked at Barnes & Noble and Half Price Books, and taught English at Harrisburg Area Community College and York College. He now lives with his wife and son in Flagstaff, Arizona, where he has been teaching composition and creative writing at Coconino Community College since 2009. Besides writing, his other passions include education, literature, nature, spirituality, space, and music. *Like a Lover Never Leaving* is his first prose book, trailing his debut poetry chapbook entitled *Catalyst*, published by Liquid Light Press in 2012. Currently, he is working on *Cardiac Orchestra*, another poetry book, and *A Quiet Revolution of the Heart*, a collection of reflections inspired by Trek III of this book.

Made in the USA
Middletown, DE
18 June 2021